A FI

El Jéfe star... Bunch's camp. Bullets ripped through tree limbs and sent splinters and sap flying, but this did nothing to slow Hughes and the others. Doc Neal went for his rifle, and King and Hunt opened up with their six-guns. Lead crisscrossed the space between El Jéfe and the camp. . . .

El Jéfe fired. It took Hughes' hat off and sent it spinning into the single large campfire blazing in the middle of their bivouac. Hughes ducked and spun, almost shooting Curly Bill in the back. The gunfighter charged wildly uphill, roaring out in defiance.

El Jéfe tried to end the gunman's life time and again. He fired and fired, but Curly Bill led a charmed existence. The bullets went wild and Bill roared on.

Slocum saw that his plan had been shot to hell and gone. He started circling, thinking he could come up on the camp from the direction of the steep canyon wall. They might not expect anyone to attack from there. This would give him ample opportunity to rescue Belicia and maybe shoot a burro or two. Dead animals couldn't carry silver. Anything left would be his to take out later.

After he'd evened the score with Hughes and the other outlaws in his gang. . . .

DON'T MISS THESE
ALL-ACTION WESTERN SERIES
FROM THE BERKLEY PUBLISHING GROUP

THE GUNSMITH by J.R. Roberts
> Clint Adams was a legend among lawmen, outlaws, and
> ladies. They called him . . . the Gunsmith.

LONGARM by Tabor Evans
> The popular long-running series about U.S. Deputy
> Marshal Long—his life, his loves, his fight for justice.

LONE STAR by Wesley Ellis
> The blazing adventures of Jessica Starbuck and the martial
> arts master, Ki. Over eight million copies in print.

SLOCUM by Jake Logan
> Today's longest-running action western. John Slocum rides
> a deadly trail of hot blood and cold steel.

JAKE LOGAN

SILVER TOWN SHOWDOWN

BERKLEY BOOKS, NEW YORK

SILVER TOWN SHOWDOWN

A Berkley Book / published by arrangement with
the author

PRINTING HISTORY
Berkley edition / August 1992

ISBN: 0-425-13359-1

A BERKLEY BOOK® TM 757,375
Berkley Books are published by The Berkley Publishing Group,
200 Madison Avenue, New York, New York 10016.
The name "BERKLEY" and the "B" logo
are trademarks belonging to Berkley Publishing Corporation.

PRINTED IN THE UNITED STATES OF AMERICA

10 9 8 7 6 5 4 3 2

1

"I want to kill something," grumbled Curly Bill. He jumped to his feet and his hand flashed to the six-shooter dangling at his side. John Slocum watched as the gun cleared leather and the hammer came back. He was the only one other than Curly Bill who didn't flinch when the heavy pistol went off with a loud report that echoed in the quiet New Mexico air like cannonade. White smoke floated lazily on the hot summer breeze and vanished slowly.

The lizard sunning itself on a rock had been blown in half, leaving only a bloody wet spot. Ants came from nowhere to begin work on both blood and carcass. For them, this was a good morning, one filled with ample food.

"That was a damn fool thing to do," growled Jim Hughes. He had tensed a mite, his hand going toward his holstered six-shooter when Curly Bill had drawn. If he'd ever cracked a smile in his life, this wasn't going to be the time. He wasn't happy with Curly Bill. "Echoes can be heard for miles. You might have scared them off."

"Ain't nobody to scare off, Hughes," Curly Bill said, turning. The six-gun hung in his hand as if he had forgotten it. Slocum watched the killer's flat, expressionless gray eyes, wondering if this was going to be the blow-off. Curly Bill hadn't liked the way Jim Hughes had been running the gang, claiming all they ever got was sore feet and no gold. Pickings had been slim but not enough to justify killing.

Slocum looked around the tight circle watching the pair and wondered if anyone else would mind Curly Bill blowing away their leader. In spite of the name, Doc Neal was hardly dry behind the ears. His long blond hair flopped in the hot breeze blowing down from the White Mountains, and his pale blue eyes showed only confusion. Zwing Hunt and Sandy King would go along with whoever was left standing. Neither had voiced an opinion in the three weeks Slocum had ridden with the Hughes Bunch.

It was Curly Bill who worried him most. The man fancied himself a gunslick, the fastest gun in the West, bar none. And Slocum had to give him this much. He was fast and his first bullet usually found its target. The dead lizard was only the most recent of his victims. Curly Bill wasn't the kind of man anyone went up against because he wanted to, and that showed in Hughes. There wasn't a trace of fear on Jim Hughes' face, but Slocum caught more than a touch of annoyance and maybe a tad of concern.

"We ain't gettin' rich ridin' with you, Hughes," Curly Bill said, too loud. He was working himself up into a killing mood. All he had to do was lift his six-shooter and he'd be right on target. Hughes had to draw, cock and fire. Considering Curly Bill's reflexes and accuracy, this wasn't as much a gunfight as it was dynamiting fish in a barrel. Jim Hughes was a dead man if lead started flying.

"Wasn't too rich before I joined up with the gang," Slocum said loudly, breaking the man's concentration enough to make him look away from Hughes. "We haven't hit it big yet, true, but so what? We're doing all right."

"Nobody asked you for your damned advice, Slocum."
Curly Bill wanted to kill someone. He'd start with Hughes,
then move to Slocum. But worry crept into his face. He was
starting to think and saw that Slocum wouldn't let him get
more than one shot off. He could cut down Hughes fine and
proper, but he'd be buried in a shallow grave alongside him.
Slocum wasn't going to sit idly by and let anyone plug him
full of holes.

As Curly Bill shifted his stance to take on Slocum first,
Hughes made his move. He stepped two paces in the other
direction, putting Curly Bill in a bad spot. He'd be in a
crossfire no matter who he went for first. His gunhand
twitched as he considered lifting the six-shooter and letting
loose at Slocum, but he kept looking over his shoulder in
Hughes' direction. No matter what he did, if he started
shooting now he'd be in a passel of trouble.

"The army payroll," Hughes reminded him in a low,
soothing voice. "They'll be coming along any time now. If
you go shooting your gun off again, they'll be sure to hear it.
You don't want to up and spook 'em now, do you, Bill?"

"Tell us about the payroll again," Slocum urged, moving
to get into still better position.

"Fort Huachuca gets paid once a month. They ship it
through this pass from Fort Bliss."

"Why don't they send it on the train?" Slocum asked,
though they had been over this time and again.

"Train tracks don't go near enough Huachucha. It's an
out-of-the-way fort. Damned near sixty men there, but not
important like Bliss or Fort Selden."

Slocum let Hughes do the rest of the explaining. He just
stood and watched Curly Bill's resolve fade. The man
had needed blood like a drunkard needs another shot of
gut-rotting whiskey, but his mood was fading fast, like ice
in the hot desert sun.

"You can use the money, Bill, to go find Wyatt Earp,
like you been meaning to do for months," Hughes rambled
on. Slocum saw this was the right thing to say. Curly Bill

wanted Earp's hide so bad he could taste it. And who was to say that the gunman might not be able to take the Arizona marshal?

"Yeah, I can do that," Curly Bill said, his hand relaxing. He thrust his six-shooter back into his holster and dropped down to poke at the ashes of their campfire. The coffee had long since gone cold, but he didn't seem to notice. He was lost in his dream of facing Earp and putting a .44 slug through the Arizona lawman's belly. "Yeah," he repeated. Then he looked up, as if he'd just awakened and realized he was surrounded by others. "How much you think we can get off that payroll shipment, Jim?"

Hughes relaxed, too. He shook his head and said, "Enough to keep us going awhile longer. I got other plans, big plans, ones that will make us all famous."

"Rather be rich," Slocum allowed. He settled back down, squatting on his haunches, sure that Curly Bill's blood passion had died for the moment. A quick look at King and Hunt showed they were only incidentally aware of how close one or two of their number had come to getting killed. Neither had anything much under their hats but hair, but they were easygoing and that suited Slocum just fine. He didn't cotton much to watching his back all the time. It was bad enough when he was around Curly Bill.

"The payroll won't do that for us, but this other job will. I assure you of that," Hughes said in his solemn way.

"What you got planned, Jim?" asked Zwing Hunt. "I can handle being rich. Fact is, the notion appeals to me in a big way."

"Tell you later," Hughes said, jumping to his feet. He held his hand up to shade his eyes as he peered into the rising sun. "There they are. A line of a dozen blue-bellies and enough greenbacks to keep us happy for a month."

"Can't keep me happy that long," Sandy King said. "I been workin' up a powerful thirst."

"Let's ride. You know where you go to get 'em in a crossfire. Don't think of changing plans now or we'll find ourselves locked up in the Yuma Penitentiary." Hughes gave this warning strictly for Curly Bill. There would be enough killing to suit even the frizzy-haired killer's blood lust, but there wasn't any reason to go out of the way to cut down a trooper. It wasn't a big enough payroll to die for. Like as not, they'd just hand over the payroll and ride on into the Arizona fort to report the theft. By then, the Hughes Bunch would be over the border and into central Mexico.

Doc Neal let out a whoop that startled Slocum and he wondered if any of them, except maybe Jim Hughes, had a lick of sense. He duplicated Hughes' action and peered into the rising sun. The horse soldiers were too far off to have heard. He made sure his saddle was cinched tight on the chestnut mare he rode, since she had a habit of puffing out her belly and then relaxing it a mile down the road. Slocum didn't want to lose his mount if there was any pursuit. He might find himself with a noose around his neck.

Robbing an army payroll was bad enough, but Slocum had already had uncounted wanted posters floating around with his likeness on them for too many years. He had returned to his family's farm in Calhoun, Georgia, after the war and tried to make a go of it, but violence followed him like flies to shit. A carpetbagger judge from Connecticut had taken a shine to the Slocum spread and decided to have it for his own. Talk had him turning it into the biggest stud farm south of Kentucky. Charges of unpaid taxes during the war were made, and the judge rode out to confiscate the place.

He'd been clever enough to bring a hired gun with him. He hadn't been clever enough to know who he was tangling with. John Slocum had ridden out that night— two new graves on the hill by the spring house— and a reward for judge-killing had dogged his steps ever since.

He would swing if they caught him. That made his life simple enough. No matter what happened, he wouldn't get caught.

He and a nervous Doc Neal positioned themselves with rifles atop boulders along the road. King and Hunt would cut off the retreat, letting the column pass them, and then move into position. Curly Bill and Hughes would do the actual robbing. Slocum had looked over the point of ambush and couldn't find a better one. Hughes had a good head when it came to planning; unfortunately, the men in his gang were seldom up to the imagination their leader showed in strategy.

The blond Doc Neal pushed back an unruly cowlick so it laid flat on his head. He rested his left elbow on his hat which he'd put on the rock for padding. He settled down and muttered to himself, carrying on both sides of a heated discussion.

Slocum was more relaxed. He had been a sniper during the war and knew how to keep calm. He went over the shot he might have to make a dozen times in his mind, figuring windage and distance and his own ability. By the time he was sure he could make the shot, the soldiers had ridden into the trap.

"Here we go," Doc Neal said, his voice almost breaking with the strain.

"No need to shoot 'less they put up a fuss," Slocum cautioned. The young Neal might not get buck fever, but Slocum wanted to keep him from making any bad mistakes. He wanted to steal the payroll and be in Mexico before anyone at the fort knew it was gone. Leaving behind a lot of dead soldiers only meant trouble later on. The army might forget a lost payroll but it would never forgive the loss of a dozen men.

The words were hardly out of Slocum's mouth when gunfire erupted below. He didn't see what happened, but he thought he could make a good guess. Curly Bill had just opened up, killing the officer at the front of the column and wounding the guidon bearer.

Slocum saw they didn't have any choice. If they wanted to even the odds, they had to ambush the other soldiers. He

started firing slowly and methodically, picking his targets
with care. The way the soldiers' horses began rearing and
shying, it wasn't a hard fight, but Slocum accounted for
three of the troopers. Curly Bill continued to blaze away
and Hughes had joined in. Doc Neal didn't fire. He just
sprawled across the rock, his left arm pinning down his hat.
From behind the column down the road came the ragged
fire of Hunt and King.

Only when the last soldier lay on the ground did the
shooting stop. Slocum cautiously stood and looked down
at the carnage. It wasn't anything he hadn't seen before.
Riding with Quantrill's Raiders had hardened him more than
anything else in his life, but this was senseless murder. The
soldiers hadn't been given the chance to fork over the payroll
before they were gunned down.

"Come on," Slocum said to Doc Neal. "We got to get out
of here. That fool Curly Bill will have us all swinging from
the limb of a cottonwood before sundown."

"I didn't shoot," the man stammered. His forehead was
liquid with sweat and his hand still shook like a leaf in a
high wind. "I watched and I froze up."

Slocum reached over and yanked the rifle from Doc Neal's
hands. He triggered the round that had been in the chamber,
levered a new round in and tossed the rifle back to him.

"Who's to know now?" Anyone checking would smell
the powder at the rifle's muzzle.

"Thanks, Slocum," Doc Neal said. "I owe you for this
one."

"Remember it, and watch my back, especially when Curly
Bill's behind me," Slocum said. He needed all the allies he
could get in the Hughes Bunch if Bill was out of control.
As he made his way down the meandering trail leading to
the main road, Slocum considered gunning Curly Bill down
like a rattler. No warning, no quarter, just getting him in his
sights and shooting him.

"What went wrong?" Slocum heard Zwing Hunt shouting
as he and King rode up from behind. "Why'd they start

shooting? I thought they was going to cave in quicklike."

Jim Hughes stood, his usual sour expression even grim-
mer. He glared at Curly Bill, who went from soldier to
soldier, robbing the dead. He lifted his pistol and aimed
it at Curly Bill's back. The hammer fell on an empty
chamber. Before Hughes could remedy the situation by
reloading, Curly Bill swung around, grinning from ear to
ear. He had his six-gun tucked into his belt where he could
draw it quickly.

"Lookee here. I got me a damn fine gold pocket
watch."

"Why not take his scalp, too?" Slocum said.

"No time," Curly Bill said, getting up. "You sound like
you don't want any part of this, Slocum. That so?"

"Where's the payroll?" Slocum didn't want to stay around
any longer than he had to. The army had patrols out all the
time looking for Apaches sneaking off their reservations.

"Got it, Slocum," said Doc Neal, holding up a canvas
pouch. It didn't look big enough for a month's pay for two
men, much less an entire fort.

"Lemme see," yelled Curly Bill. He ran over and grabbed
the pouch from Neal's hand. Ripping it open with a nicked
knife, he dumped the contents into the dust.

"Chicken feed," he grumbled. "That's all this is. Hell
if there's more'n twenty dollars apiece—and it's all in
greenbacks. Nothing but scrip. Worthless paper money!"
He grabbed a handful of bills and tossed them high into
the air. King and Hunt went scrambling for the fluttering
sheets.

"Give me my share and I'll be out of here," Slocum said.
"I don't care how much it is."

"Wait, you can't cut and run like that, Slocum. We got
plans. Big ones. Down in Mexico," protested Hughes. The
outlaw looked from Slocum to Curly Bill and back. The
others were with him, no matter what he did. To them
nothing much mattered.

"*You've* got plans. I just want to keep my hide in one

piece." He eyed Curly Bill so Hughes would get his drift.

"Let's go divvy up the money where it's safe. You know how the cavalry patrols." Hughes wasn't begging. He would die before he did that, but Slocum saw something in the man's eye that held his attention.

"The job," Slocum said suddenly. "Is it really good?"

"Yeah," Jim Hughes said, grinning from ear to ear. That convinced Slocum it was worth his time. Hughes never smiled. This had to be better than just good. It had to be the crime of the century.

2

"Wasn't enough."

Slocum looked over at Curly Bill and wondered what was going on behind those slate-gray eyes. He wasn't sure he wanted to know, not really. The cavalry payroll robbery had brought them each less than twenty dollars, and it had been in almost worthless greenbacks. No self-respecting barkeep would take scrip for a drink without discounting the paper by half. With any luck—or with a bartender who was sampling his own wares—Slocum knew they might be able to buy a bottle of whiskey each and not much more.

A bottle of whiskey apiece and twelve dead troopers. The more he thought about the slaughtered soldiers, the more his resolve to leave the Hughes Bunch hardened. Jim Hughes was all right, Doc Neal, too. But the others were just taking up space.

And then there was Curly Bill. Slocum had seen his share of killers who seemed more like mad dogs than humans. Bill was taking on every aspect of a rabid dog except frothing at the mouth. Waiting around for that to happen wasn't in the

10

cards. It was better to just ride on out when nobody was looking.

"John, I need a word with you," Hughes said. Slocum looked up from where he rested, his hat pulled down to shade his eyes from the setting sun. They had ridden hard that day and he was tuckered out. But a man couldn't ride deep enough into the desert to get away from the U.S. Army when they discovered their slain comrades.

"Could have been more," Slocum said, trying to find the right excuse to just leave without getting Hughes' dander up.

"Don't go. This is going to be a big job, and I'll need you for it." Hughes almost smiled again. Slocum tried to remember the number of times he'd seen the outlaw grin and had trouble. But every time Hughes thought of this elusive job the corners of his mouth twitched in just the right direction.

That intrigued Slocum enough to stay around—for a spell.

"What is it? You're going to have to tell us sooner or later."

"I'm worried about Curly Bill. I looked to him as my second-in-command, leastwise I did until you showed up."

"I'm not looking to take over." The last thing Slocum wanted was a feud over control in the gang. He either agreed with what Jim Hughes planned or he didn't. If he didn't, he'd be gone like the hot desert wind. Getting into a fight with Curly Bill over something he didn't even want struck Slocum as ridiculous *and* dangerous.

"Didn't say you were, but Bill is leaning that way. He's a suspicious cayuse."

"He's a cold-blooded killer." Slocum killed when he had to, but he shied away from those who enjoyed spilling blood. He'd gotten a bellyful of that during the war. Bloody Bill Anderson and Quantrill and even Quantrill's wife, Kate, had gotten a thrill out of murdering and maiming and making people suffer.

"I know what he is," Hughes said, his mouth in a tight line. "But I need him, too. I need the lot of you for this."

"So?"

"Stick with me. Just another couple days. That's all I'm asking. We got to meet some folks down in Mexico and talk over details with them, then we'll be richer than your dreams ever made you."

"That's a powerful lot of gold," Slocum allowed. "I've had plenty of time to think on such things."

"More," Hughes assured him. "A mountain more."

"All right," Slocum said, intrigued. His curiosity bump often got him into a world of trouble, but he knew the dangers riding with the Hughes Bunch. If he didn't turn his back on Curly Bill, he'd be all right. The man was fast, but Slocum wasn't sure if he wasn't just a tad faster and a whole lot more accurate.

"There's more, another reason I need you," Hughes said, his eyes beginning to glow with excitement. "I need somebody who can palaver with the Mexicans. You know the lingo, don't you?"

"I rode with some *ladrinos* out of Nuevo Laredo for a spell," Slocum admitted. "I picked up enough to get by."

Hughes nodded and began rubbing his hands together. "I want you there with me tomorrow instead of Curly Bill. And don't let on you know a word of Spanish."

"I'm supposed to spy on somebody?" Slocum didn't like this. Nobody ever trusted anybody else, and that was all right, but Slocum didn't cotton to the idea of sneaking around and putting his ear to doors.

"Not exactly. Me and El Jéfe get along okay, but if he starts talking native to his men, I want to know."

"You suspecting a trap?"

"Maybe," Hughes said. "I just don't trust 'em too much, not with so much at stake. If they're talking behind my back, I want to know exactly what they're saying."

Slocum nodded. He saw that he wasn't going to get any more information from Hughes until the meeting began, and then he might get more by eavesdropping than straight from the outlaw. He sank back and adjusted his hat to shield his eyes from the rays of the dying sun and drifted off to a fitful sleep plagued by dreams of Curly Bill and the flashing speed of his quick draw.

He came awake instantly, hand going to the Colt Navy in his cross-draw holster. For a few seconds he didn't know what had spooked him. Then he heard the horses nickering softly. Something bothered them. He rose, drawing his ebony-handled six-shooter and making a quick judgment of time by the position of the stars.

"Slocum, good, you're up. Saddle your horse. We got to get to town by dawn. That's when we're supposed to meet El Jéfe."

"Who is this El Jéfe? Every tin-plated bandito along the border calls himself the Chief."

"El Jéfe has a gang you might have heard of. *Los Bandidos de la Estrada* they call themselves."

"Maybe I have heard of them," Slocum said. "Bandits of the Road" was a common enough name for a gang, but there had been a few well-planned bank robberies in Tombstone and El Paso that might have been committed by this gang.

"El Jéfe thinks big, I'll give him that. You saddled and ready?"

"Are we just leaving the others?" asked Slocum.

"They know what I have to do. They'll stick around awhile. Maybe Curly Bill will get antsy and ride on."

"He'd go straight for Tombstone and Earp," Slocum said.

"Might be the best that could happen for us all," Hughes said. "They'll be here a spell. If we don't get back by tomorrow night, then they'll know something went wrong."

Slocum didn't like the idea of just riding off and not talking with the others. There had to be some trust in a group, even a band of desperate outlaws, but Hughes didn't seem to worry. And Slocum knew he could keep riding on into Mexico if things turned sour. He didn't have to talk with El Jéfe.

"How do we work this? Are we together or do I ride in alone and let them think we don't know each other?"

Hughes shook his head. "They know I'm bringing some-one with me. And no gringo will be allowed in Las Moscas without El Jéfe's approval. We're together and you just hang back and listen hard. Me and El Jéfe will do all the planning."

"For what?" Slocum asked as they rode due south across the New Mexico border and into Mexico. Las Moscas was more than fifteen miles off. Even riding hard, they'd reach it after sunrise. Slocum didn't like the idea they'd be exhausted from the trip and the Estrada Gang would be rested and ready for any treachery.

"Can't tell you yet, not until me and El Jéfe agree on some details. We'll be walking away with a mountain of silver."

"This isn't some map to the Lost Dutchman Mine, is it?" Slocum snorted and almost told Hughes what he thought of such a harebrained scheme. He touched his vest pocket. Four silver ten peso pieces rode there. He didn't know for certain, but it was a good bet that the coins were more than any treasure hunt would bring him.

"This isn't any wild goose chase. El Jéfe says we can do it, his gang and the Hughes Bunch together. It's that big. I want to listen to the entire plan one last time, then decide if it's really possible." Hughes smiled again. Slocum knew he'd gotten as much as he was likely to from the dour outlaw, but Hughes liked the idea of so much silver. He smiled. He actually smiled.

That counted for a whale of a lot.

They rode fast and hard for endless hours until Slocum was about ready to drop from exhaustion. His chest-nut mare was lathered and her sides heaved. He was getting ready to tell Hughes to go on without him so he could rest his mount when the outlaw leader pointed.

"Las Moscas. We made it with a few minutes to spare." The sun had poked above the horizon, turning the Sonora Desert stifling and deadly. Another hour would make travel impossible.

"A cool beer would go down good right now," Hughes said.

"There," Slocum said. "The cantina. A half dozen horses out back. El Jéfe is waiting for us."

"Let him wait another few minutes," Hughes said. Slocum saw the calculation on the man's face. "It'll keep him honest—or as honest as he can be. Let's tend to the horses."

Slocum knew this was as much a matter of their survival as common decency toward the valiant horses. A rested animal might get them out of trouble if El Jéfe turned against them. As tuckered out as the horses were from the night's hard travel, a race into the desert's heat would leave them dead within a mile.

They rode slowly into the sleepy Mexican border town. No one was in sight, but Slocum felt someone's eyes following them. They dismounted in front of a simple livery stable. The wide-eyed boy didn't speak English, but Slocum used sign language and one of his precious silver ten-peso pieces to get his message across. The horses would be well tended for such a magnificent sum.

"Let's go find El Jéfe," Hughes said, settling his gunbelt around his middle. Slocum followed his lead and released the leather thong looped over the hammer of his Colt Navy. He didn't bother loading the sixth cylinder; he always rode with the hammer on an empty cylinder to keep from shooting off his own leg. If five rounds didn't suffice, the sixth wouldn't matter much, he decided.

"He's already found us," Slocum said, his green eyes cold and hard on the tall man filling the door of the cantina. Faded gold-thread embroidery work decorated a tattered jacket. Bandoliers crossed his broad chest and twin pistols were hung in cross-draw holsters at his sides. He held a short carbine in hands so large they could engulf the top of a man's head.

"That's his number two man," Hughes said. "Don't pay him any mind."

Slocum stared up from his six-foot height into the monstrous bandido's brown eyes and saw no emotion there. Curly Bill was bad but he could be handled. He hoped he never had to cross this one. Bill was a blow-hard, for all his skill with a pistol. Slocum wasn't sure what it would take to bring down this Mexican.

Hughes pushed past. Slocum followed, aware of the eyes boring into his back. But for all the bandido's size, he wasn't as intimidating as El Jéfe. The Mexican outlaw sat at a table by himself. The others in the cantina rode with him, of that Slocum was sure. They had the hard-bitten look of men used to living by wit and rifle.

"Ah, Señor Hughes, you have decided to come."

"Had a few chores to tend to, El Jéfe," Hughes said, sitting across the table from the Mexican highwayman.

"I have heard. The United States Cavalry is not so pleased with you at this moment. Was it needed to kill them all to rob such a small payroll?"

Slocum heard the criticism laced in the man's joking words. El Jéfe's mouth smiled, but his eyes didn't. He pushed a bottle of fiery tequila toward Hughes in silent invitation. Obviously the Mexican leader always heard of anything unusual along the border to know so quickly of yesterday's robbery.

Hughes knocked back a shot of tequila, then poured himself another. Slocum watched carefully as Hughes gauged how much of the potent liquor he could handle and how much El Jéfe might have consumed. In spite of the bottle being almost empty, both Hughes and Slocum knew the bandit chieftain hadn't been drinking. He had been waiting, a spider in the center of his web waiting for his prey. If the gringos got roaring drunk, that was their business.

"Good," Hughes said, his voice choked from the alcohol. "I prefer that other stuff. What do you call it? The stuff with the worm in the bottom?"

"Mescal," El Jéfe said. "This is a poor town, Las Moscas. There is none to be had. No pulque, either. But there will be much for us when we do this robbery, eh?"

Slocum settled down into a chair behind Hughes. He hadn't been offered any tequila and didn't make a move to take any. The byplay between Hughes and El Jéfe was like a bullfighter feeling out a bull: a deft move here, a sweeping motion there, and let the horns slide past harmlessly. Slocum leaned back and closed his eyes, listening to the men who rode with El Jéfe. They spoke in low voices, in Spanish. Much of what they said was inconsequential. Only when El Jéfe relaxed a little and began talking with Hughes in more detail of the robbery did they start to discuss Hughes and Slocum.

Slocum wanted to listen to El Jéfe and find out for certain what was going on. He heard him mention Monterrey and pack burros and guano. None of it made any sense, but Hughes grew more animated as the Mexican bandit chief spoke. Slocum found his attention turning to the others in *Los Bandidos de la Estrada.*

They were even more excited than their leader about the robbery, and not a one of them seemed to think it was impossible to become rich.

Very rich.

Slocum caught mention of the town of Monterrey over and over as they spoke rapid-fire Spanish. Nothing he heard warned him of a double-cross. The Mexicans needed the American outlaws for the robbery; of that much he was convinced. He couldn't figure out why they didn't simply recruit more of their own countrymen if they wanted a small army. But they were eager to have the Hughes Bunch join with them.

"Hughes, you be needing me for awhile?" he asked.

Hughes motioned him away. "I need to talk some

more with El Jéfe." Hughes turned and looked at him a moment, remembering why he'd brought Slocum along. Worry crossed Hughes' face.

"Everything's fine," Slocum reassured him. "I just need to get myself into a bath and soak off some trail dirt. I don't reckon you'll be needing me." He saw relief pour into Jim Hughes. Then the man turned dour once more.

"Go take your damned bath," Hughes said, "but be ready to go fetch the others when I tell you. Things are moving fast. There's going to be more silver than a hundred men can spend in a lifetime when we pull off this robbery."

"Don't expect to be long," Slocum answered. He rose and left the cantina, passing the huge guard at the door. This time the man smiled to show he accepted Slocum as a partner in the holdup. Even so, Slocum shivered as he left. Some men should never smile.

3

Slocum still didn't know much about this grand robbery, but he had heard enough to understand Hughes would be telling him a lot more about it soon. Right now he ached from the all-night ride and needed to get some of the trail dust off. He stretched and yawned, then looked around Las Moscas. There didn't seem to be much in the way of hotel or barber shops. Slocum began wandering, aware of the eyes following him. Gringos passed through this border town, but that was all they did. Everyone knew he and Hughes had arrived to talk to El Jéfe.

What El Jéfe and his *Los Bandidos de la Estrada* might have done to the town wasn't something Slocum wanted to discover. The bands of outlaws roaming the border usually preyed on the *peones* and kept them poor and scared.

Still, El Jéfe had mentioned Monterrey and that was a rich city, full of life and trade and more opportunity than anything along the New Mexico Territory–Mexico border. Slocum walked to the edge of town and stared out across the desert. There wasn't a drop of water in sight, but he knew Las Moscas couldn't exist without getting water from somewhere. He circled the town and fifteen minutes later came upon a small oasis. A spring bubbled up from the ground and drained into a large pool that supplied the town's water.

But Slocum wasn't interested in this as much as he was a small baked adobe trough that led away from the town and meandered downhill. Someone below sang with a soft, melodious voice that drew him. Slocum stopped and just stared for a moment when he saw the large tub under the trough. Water trickled down in a small shower that left bright, sunlit droplets of moisture on the nut-brown skin of the most gorgeous woman Slocum had seen in years.

She bathed, lathering her body with slow, sensual strokes. She turned slightly, showing her profile. Firm, high breasts jutted from her chest. The water must be colder than Slocum imagined because the woman's nipples had hardened into coppery points. She sang a lullaby as she scrubbed.

Slocum felt himself responding to the sight of the woman bending over when she dropped the small bar of soap she used. Her buttocks were round and firm, and it had been too long since he'd been with a woman, much less one this lovely.

She tossed her head back and sent water flying. She stroked the long, black tresses and then turned back in his direction. Their eyes met, her chocolate ones staring unashamedly into his green. She made no move to hide her nakedness.

"Excuse me, ma'am," Slocum said. "Didn't mean to intrude. I was just looking for a place to take a bath myself." He turned away, sorry to lose such a fine sight, but it wouldn't do to tangle with the locals over a woman. Jim Hughes was convinced the robbery down in Monterrey was going to make them rich. Riling up everyone in Las Moscas—and probably El Jéfe—might jinx the chance to see more than a couple coins in his pocket.

"Wait, don't go. You are the *Americano* who came with Hughes, aren't you?"

Slocum turned back and stared at her. "How'd you know that?"

"I am Belicia," she said, her voice reaching out and caressing Slocum like a lover's soft touch. "Belicia Salazar."

"Pleased to see you," Slocum said, smiling. Belicia still made no move to cover herself, even though Slocum saw a large wool blanket beside the tub.

"What is your name?" she asked, still unabashedly naked under the trickle of water from the trough a few inches above her head.

"John Slocum."

"Pleased to meet you, Mr. Slocum." She smiled and dimples showed, though Slocum had a time of it keeping his eyes locked on hers. Every movement she made caused the sunlight to catch another drop of water and send new rays off her sleek body in a million rainbows.

"Better go." Again he turned reluctantly to leave. Any woman this bold had a protector in the village. Slocum didn't want to lock horns with him, not when Hughes and El Jéfe were finishing their plans for the big robbery.

"You are going to Monterrey for the silver?"

This stopped Slocum dead in his tracks. He turned and looked at her. She smiled, her even white teeth gleaming. She was mocking him.

"What do you know about Monterrey?"

"I know many things of the city. Come, scrub my back and I will tell you. It is a rich city, one filled with more wealth than a dozen men could spend in their lifetime, even if they lived to be very, very old." She turned her brown back to him and held out a wash cloth. "Do not use too much of the soap. It burns my skin. Do you see?"

"I see," Slocum said, taking the lye soap and rubbing it across the cloth Belicia had been using. She purred like a cat when he began washing her back. She didn't seem to mind when he worked across her shoulders, then moved lower to the small of her back and finished on those round, tight buttocks.

"You are very good at this. What else are you good at?"

"I know a thing or two about—" This was as far as Slocum got before she turned and he found himself with an armful of wet, wanton woman. She kissed him hard and made him forget all he had been thinking, about how she must have a powerful protector in Las Moscas. What the hell did it matter to him? He was leaving town soon, and Belicia was more than willing.

She broke off the kiss and took a half step back in the tub, almost losing her balance. "You kiss very well. What other abilities do you have?" Her hand rushed across the bulge just under his belt buckle. Fire swept through Slocum's loins and burned out the last trace of caution. He unfastened his gunbelt and tossed it aside. He felt her nimble fingers working on his clothing. He kicked free of his boots and stepped into the tub with Belicia as she skinned him out of his shirt and started working on his trousers.

"You need a bath," she said, making a face. Her hands caressed his body. Slocum got harder by the second until he felt like a stick of dynamite waiting to explode. He groaned as she dropped to her knees and worked her face across his groin. Hot lips brushed the tip of his manhood and teased it into a steely spike.

"Don't," he gasped out. He tossed his head back to get the water from his eyes. The cool water dripping from the trough would have been enough for him. He hadn't bargained on finding such a lovely and agreeable woman.

"You do not like Belicia's lips?"

She closed her mouth around his rigid length and turned him weak in the knees. Slocum fought to keep himself under control. There was so much more he wanted from her, to share with her. He reached out, as much for support as to explore her lush body.

His fingers touched the hard nubbins at the tips of her breasts. Belicia let out a tiny sigh of enjoyment. She rose slowly, pressing wetly against him until she stood, her face upturned for another kiss. He gave it to her. His hands reached around to cup her rump and pull her even closer. Then his fingers parted the half moons and explored the dampness between her thighs.

She sighed again, widening her stance enough to allow a finger to slide into her interior. He began moving his middle finger in and out of the tightness.

"It is nice, John, but there must be more," she said. Belicia curled a leg around his waist and did a little crow hop to get still closer. She opened herself completely to him doing this. Her hand closed on him and guided the thickness to the spot where his finger had been.

They melted together, hot sun beating down, cool water dripping over them, their groins joined. Slocum felt her breasts crushed against his chest, her suppleness moving slowly around him, her lips questing for his. He hadn't wanted to come to Las Moscas with Hughes. Now he was glad Hughes had chosen him rather than Curly Bill.

They kissed long and deep, their tongues playing hide and seek. Slocum tried to keep still and let the woman move since he didn't trust his own body, but he quickly found he couldn't do that. The urgency mounting within denied him prolonged pleasure. He cupped her buttocks and lifted her entirely out of the tub, then began bouncing her up and down on his long shaft.

The friction mounted quickly and Belicia soon moaned like a mournful coyote, shuddering as she did. She clung frantically to him, her fingernails cutting into his flesh. Slocum hardly noticed. White hot fire lanced upward as he spilled his seed into her. He rocked back and forth, keeping the woman's body moving until there was nothing left for either of them.

Belicia slipped to her knees in the large tub again. She pulled him down beside her.

"Now, let us finish our bath," she said almost primly.

"Who are you?" Slocum asked. "What do you know about Monterrey?"

Belicia Salazar laughed and the sound was like wind in the high pines, silver bells, the most lovely music Slocum had ever heard.

"The mint at Monterrey. The Mexican National Mint. El Jéfe intends to rob it."

"How do you know this?"

Again Belicia laughed, but her answer turned Slocum cold inside. "I know this because I ride with El Jéfe."

4

"Do not look so surprised. Who else do you think gets such luxury?" Belicia held her hand under the falling water.

"This isn't going to cause any trouble?" Slocum was already fumbling to get into his clothes and be sure his ebony-handled Colt was ready for action.

"There is no trouble. I enjoyed it. Did you?" She batted her long dark eyelashes and smiled coyly at him. Slocum kept from cursing. Women like this made for a lot of dead men. They teased and cajoled and made men fight over them. Then they stood by and laughed when the bullets began flying.

"I don't think El Jéfe is the kind who likes to share anything that's his."

Belicia laughed at this. "José can be possessive, but be is a good man. He is not the animal you think." Some fire returned to her eyes when she added, "And I am *not* a piece of property. José does *not* own me."

Slocum remembered the huge bandido filling the canti-na doorway. El Jéfe—José—might not be a cold-blooded murderer but he surrounded himself with them. He hadn't come to lead the Estrada Gang because he was kind to small animals.

"You worry so, John. Do not. I wanted what happened. Nothing will be said of this to José, unless you are the one to brag." She watched him carefully, as if wondering whether he would boast to El Jéfe that he'd just had his woman.

"I don't want trouble."

"You want only the money."

Slocum stared at her in amazement. Belicia sounded as if the money didn't matter much to her. For the first time, Slocum wasn't entirely blinded by her beauty. He looked closely and saw she was no peon. Those hands had never seen hard labor. Nothing had coarsened her features. Long hours toiling in the sun were alien to her. But she didn't seem the pampered hothouse flower so common on ranchos south of the border. The contrasts and the mystery she presented intrigued Slocum even more.

"That's a powerful attraction," Slocum allowed, tightening his gunbelt and settling the Colt on his left hip until it felt just right. He pulled on his boots and watched as Belicia started dressing. This was almost as much fun as being with her in the tub.

"You do not believe me when I said El Jéfe intends to rob the national mint?"

Slocum was still startled at the notion. The mint had more soldiers guarding it than Porfirio Diaz's presidential palace. Monterrey was a financial center and fabulously rich. The coins struck in Monterrey spread throughout Mexico. Slocum touched the silver ten peso pieces in his vest pocket. They had probably been minted in Monterrey. The Mexican government wasn't likely to let a ragtag band like El Jéfe's just walk in and take all the silver they wanted.

And the mere sight of the Hughes Bunch would bring out the *Federales* in droves.

"You have a look of disbelief." Belicia tossed her shining, dark wet hair and continued dressing, as if his opinion meant nothing to her. And it probably didn't. She was willful and used to getting what she wanted. No matter what Slocum said or did, it just didn't affect her closed world. This reinforced his guess that she was the daughter of a rich ranchero.

Why was she riding with El Jéfe?

"What I think isn't important. I'll go along with whatever Jim Hughes says."

"You do not have the look of a follower," was all she said before pulling on sandals and walking off without a backward glance at him. Slocum let her go. It wouldn't do to be seen even walking with her. As it was, Slocum wondered why El Jéfe hadn't sent along a couple of his men to guard her during her morning bath.

He checked his pistol, loading the sixth cylinder. He hadn't thought the spare round would be important. Now he wasn't so sure. After ten minutes, Slocum returned to the cantina. That mountain of a bandido still guarded the door. Slocum tried not to shudder as he pushed past into the dimness of the tiny room. Those huge hands could snap a man's neck like a farmer wringing a chicken's.

"John, glad you got back. Me and El Jéfe got everything worked out. We decided we're gonna be rich." Hughes slurred his words badly. Slocum saw two empty tequila bottles on the table and wondered if Hughes had polished off both of them. El Jéfe didn't seem any the worse for their drinking, but when Slocum left he had been plying Hughes with the liquor to loosen his tongue.

"Lemme tell you all about it." Hughes' breath was strong enough to knock over a mule. He reached over and put his arm around Slocum's shoulder, pulling him down to the chair. Slocum was aware of how closely El Jéfe watched him. He had seen vultures eyeing something ready to die in the same way.

"You are a good man, Slocum," El Jéfe said. "Hughes speaks well of you."

Slocum heard two others in El Jéfe's gang snicker at this. Slocum wasn't sure what had been said or if Hughes had

let the cat out of the bag—that Slocum understood enough
Spanish to get by. From the rapid-fire talk going on around
him, Slocum thought his secret was safe. They spoke of the
stupidity of gringos and how greedy they always were.

Slocum wasn't in any position to challenge them on the
point even if he had wanted.

"What are we going to do that we need so many men?"
Slocum tipped his head slightly to indicate the others in the
room. "A stagecoach or even a train isn't going to carry
enough to split ten or fifteen ways."

"Your concern is well placed," El Jéfe said, enjoying his
little drama. Slocum wanted to blurt out that he already
knew their target, but he held his tongue. That was a good
way of being sure they didn't separate his head from his
shoulders with one of the large machetes two of the bandidos
carried.

"Why do you need us?" Slocum asked, playing along for
the time. He was aware that any rebellion on his part might
put both him and Hughes into shallow graves. If he didn't
like the way the plan was laid out, and he didn't think he
would, all he had to do was keep riding when he left Las
Moscas. He could be in Santa Fe in a week and Denver by
the end of the month.

"We need a way of getting the silver from the mint because
there will be so much." El Jéfe laughed and then belched
loudly. For the first time Slocum knew the bandido leader
had been drinking as heavily as Hughes. The difference was
in his tolerance for the fiery tequila.

"Why us?"

"You have a mind that never lets loose, eh?" El Jéfe
belched again and drank more of the tequila before answer-
ing. "There will be great need for mules or burros. You will
steal them from your U.S. Army fort just across the border.
We will need twenty or thirty."

"And what then?"

"Guano," Hughes said, as if this was a secret. "We'll be
guano merchants. El Jéfe has it all arranged. We take the

burros to this little town, load 'em with guano and then dance on into Monterrey." He tried to snap his fingers.

In spite of himself, Slocum was intent on the plot. He didn't want anything to do with El Jéfe, yet the lure of so much silver called to him. Greed was no excuse for getting himself killed, but Slocum decided it didn't hurt to listen. Just listen. A few minutes more.

"We show up with thirty burros loaded with guano," El Jéfe said. "Everyone sees guano merchants from north of the border all the time and they don't get suspicious. We dump the guano and have pack animals for getting the silver out of town." Greed flared more brightly than ever. Thirty loads of silver and each burro might be able to carry two hundred pounds.

Three tons of silver.

Enough for everyone, no double-crossing needed.

"Twelve of us," El Jéfe went on. "Six of you, six *Los Bandidos de la Estrada.* Five hundred pounds of silver for each of us."

Slocum almost asked about Belicia's stake in the robbery but quickly bit back the words. He was all too aware of the bandidos in the room and El Jéfe's command over them.

"Sounds good," Slocum said slowly. "Too good to be true. There's got to be a garrison of soldiers."

"*Los soldados, sí,*" he said. "They will be our worry. You will get the burros into town and position yourselves near the mint. We will take care of the *soldados.*" El Jéfe laughed loudly and wiped his lips. "You do not want to share in our riches?"

"It's hard to swallow that we could get out of town with so much silver," Slocum said.

"We can do it," El Jéfe assured him. "This is not something that has just come to me. I have worked long in planning. Ask them, ask any of them!" He swept his arm around the room to indicate his men. All Slocum saw were broad smiles and outlaws fingering their weapons, as if they'd as soon cut him down as ride with him.

This was a part of the scheme that Slocum didn't like, but so much silver was a lure no man could resist.

"José?"

Slocum turned and saw Belicia standing silhouetted in the doorway. His heart came into his throat. He shifted slightly, getting his pistol ready. He didn't know what to expect from her, but it might be the worst.

"Ah, *bonita* Belicia, come in. Meet our honored guests." Something about the tone the Mexican bandit used when talking to Belicia put Slocum on his guard. El Jéfe introduced Hughes who grunted, his eyes half-hooded from too much liquor. "And this is Señor Slocum."

"Pleased to meet you," she said. Her eyes danced but she said no more. For that Slocum was glad. El Jéfe watched them both like a hawk waiting to swoop on its prey. Slocum wondered at Belicia's position with the Estrada Gang. She didn't seem to be an ordinary camp follower, though she had said she rode with El Jéfe. There was something more in her attitude that bothered Slocum. It was as if she was a prisoner, but what prisoner was allowed to go off unguarded to take a shower—and to make love with a stranger?

"She going with you?" Slocum asked.

"She is my woman," El Jéfe said, but again Slocum caught undercurrents that made him wary.

"This isn't any place for a woman," Slocum pressed. "She'll slow us down."

"She is necessary for our part of the robbery," El Jéfe said. "There will be no discussion on this part. Is that not so, Hughes?"

"Right, El Jéfe," Hughes said, slurring his words.

Slocum had been put in his place as hired gun. He settled back in his chair, watching the Mexicans. They no longer chattered among themselves now that Belicia had entered. It was as if they didn't trust themselves to speak in her presence. All this added to the gut feeling Slocum had that he and Hughes didn't know enough about the Estradas, their leader, Belicia or the Monterrey robbery.

"You will cross the border and steal the burros. We will rendezvous in Monterrey in ten days. By this time there will be enough time for you to load the guano and have established yourselves as honored merchants traveling south on business, eh?"

"Lemme have a word with Slocum, will you, El Jéfe?"

The Mexican motioned Hughes from the cantina like a king dismissing a servant. Hughes took Slocum by the elbow and steered him past the huge bandido guarding the door. Only when they were in the middle of the dusty street that ran through the center of Las Moscas did Hughes speak. Slocum was glad to hear that Hughes was nowhere near as drunk as he had appeared inside.

"We got a slight problem here, John," Hughes said earnestly. "I don't trust El Jéfe, not entirely."

"What's wrong?"

"Can't say he's fixin' to double-cross us, but that much silver is a powerful temptation."

Slocum had to agree. He wanted to forget the whole matter, but five hundred pounds of silver, if the deal was on the up-and-up, was too much to fold any hand on. Better to bluff to the end of the game.

"Me and the rest of the boys can get the burros. Stealing them won't be much of a problem."

"Fort Huachucha?" Slocum asked. "They'll be riled at losing their pay. They might even be posting guards now."

"There are a couple other places we can hit. There's an army supply depot not ten miles on the other side of the border. It's hardly more than a corral and has enough pack animals for us."

"What do you want me to do?"

"Stay with El Jéfe. I don't trust him, but we got to play along. I figure if this is a good plan, he does need us, and we need him. He won't tell how he plans to get rid of the garrison stationed at the mint. Without that little element, the whole scheme turns into suicide."

Slocum had to agree. The Mexican government was more likely to station a full company of guards there than any place else this side of Monterrey. Even a dozen men couldn't fight through fifty or more soldiers.

"You ride with him, keep him honest, and keep your eyes peeled for any dirty dealing."

"I'll join up with the rest of you in Monterrey?"

"Stick with El Jéfe. Get word to me if there's any double-cross."

Slocum considered this from ten different angles. Sweat beaded on his forehead from the blazing sun. He was going to be riding into the jaws of a trap if El Jéfe meant to do them out of their share of the silver, but the Mexican leader had come to Hughes, not the other way around. That meant the bandidos needed them and their pack animals. Not much would happen until after the robbery.

"All right," Slocum said, damning himself as a complete fool. "But I cut and run if it looks as if El Jéfe is planning anything against us."

"That's fair, John," Hughes said. He hitched his belt, lowered his eyelids and once more looked completely soused. "Let's go back and tell El Jéfe what we decided."

They reentered the cantina and sat down. Belicia stood behind El Jéfe, a hand on his shoulder. She gave Slocum a smile that was more than friendly. He tried to ignore it. Was he getting himself involved in this because of greed or his gonads? Either might get him killed.

And either might be worth any risk. Belicia Salazar was one fine-looking woman. And a quarter ton of silver would make him rich for the rest of his life, even if he lived to be a hundred.

"Slocum here will ride on down with you. If you want, you can send one of your boys up north with me."

"I need all my men to take out the mint guards," El Jéfe said. He frowned and looked hard at Slocum. "Why do you not trust me, my good friend? Is it needed that he accompany me?"

"I *do* trust you, amigo," said Hughes, pouring another shot from the tequila bottle. "Let's drink to seal the deal."

"But Slocum . . ." protested El Jéfe.

"He can be useful, José," said Belicia, her eyes dancing. "Let him come with us. What harm can there be?"

"None," El Jéfe said almost sullenly. He knocked back the shot of tequila and stood, kicking back the chair. "Come. Let us ride south now. ¡*Vámanos!*"

Slocum took a deep breath when he saw the coldness in the bandit leader's eyes. And he took another one when he saw the desire in Belicia's. He followed them into the hot noonday sun to begin the long trip to Monterrey and three tons of silver.

5

"Too risky," Slocum said. "Why rile up the *Federales* when it's the mint we're going to rob?"

El Jéfe laughed uproariously. Slocum didn't see what was so funny. The bandido wanted to rob a train for, as far as Slocum could see, the thrill of it. To get the law down on them before a big robbery was a sure ticket to a Mexican jail. Even worse, to Slocum's way of thinking, they had spent almost a week getting the lay of the land for the robbery. He wanted to ride straight for the mint and get on with that theft. Sticking up a train was a waste of precious time.

"What is the difference, eh?" El Jéfe laughed again, enjoying his attempt at philosophy. Slocum looked past him to Belicia, who rode on the outlaw's far side. She had occasionally smiled in his direction and had winked lewdly more than once during the last week, but Slocum had pretended not to notice. El Jéfe wasn't the kind of man to cross when it came to anything or anyone he considered his property, and Slocum had yet to figure out what the bandido's relationship was with the lovely woman. At times he spoke lovingly to her and at others he completely ignored her.

Even more confusing, she acted as if El Jéfe didn't exist. Belicia would look straight through him as if he had turned into a windowpane. Only when she was teasing Slocum and trying to elicit a reaction did she direct any words to the bandido.

"The difference is getting caught doing a robbery that's not necessary. If the mint is such a big job, there's no reason to muddy the water before we do it."

"You do not understand us, Señor Slocum," El Jéfe said. "What is death for ones such as we? Everything is inevitable. If we are meant to get killed robbing Monterrey, then we will. If not, so?" He shrugged eloquently, showing his disdain. "It is fated and there is nothing to be done for it."

Slocum said nothing as El Jéfe directed his small band of robbers toward the railroad tracks. They pushed a few rocks onto the tracks to stop the train. Two of them, including Paco, the mountain of a man who seemed to be El Jéfe's second-in-command, climbed onto a cliff above the spot where the train would have to stop.

"You approve of our plan?"

"Looks all right," Slocum said, still worrying about robbing the train.

"There is the smoke from the locomotive," Belicia cried. She stood in the stirrups of her saddle and pointed. Slocum saw the faint black smoke moving across the horizon. The train struggled to make the steep grade. At another time and situation, he would have gone along with the robbery. Now it seemed reckless and downright foolish in the face of a bigger plum to be picked in Monterrey.

The robbery went well, as far as Slocum could tell. A minimum of violence was needed. Once the train's engineer pulled to a screeching, spark-filled stop, the bandidos showed their rifles and flashed the thick-bladed machetes in the air. Blowing open the puny safe in the mail car took only a few seconds and resulted in a single canvas bag.

"This will do, eh?" El Jéfe said with some satisfaction. The hulking bandido rode up waving the sack in his hand.

"Give it to Belicia," El Jéfe ordered. "And let us ride!" He put his flashing silver spurs to his horse's flanks and raced off. Slocum lingered for a moment, watching Belicia. She struggled with the sack and then got it secured on the saddle in front of her.

"It will work out, John," she said softly. "Later. We will talk about this later."

Slocum glanced uncomfortably toward the giant and his machete. He didn't want this enormous bandido telling his leader there was anything between Belicia and the gringo.

"Paco will say nothing," Belicia assured him. "He has no tongue. Diaz's *Federales* cut it out when he refused to reveal José's hideout. He is loyal."

"I'm sure," Slocum said, wondering to whom Paco was most loyal, El Jéfe or Belicia. Either way spelled trouble if Slocum wasn't very careful. He was growing sorrier by the minute that he had agreed to Hughes' plan to ride along and keep El Jéfe honest in his part of the robbery.

Slocum rode along in silence, aware of Belicia and Paco on either side. He felt like a prisoner, even if they had let him keep his Colt and rifle. An hour later, El Jéfe called a halt to their flight.

"Dismount, eat, drink, rest. It will soon be siesta time," the bandido called loudly to his men. "And you, Belicia, count the money. Tell us how well we have done this morning."

Slocum watched as Belicia opened the canvas bag and began counting the money inside. El Jéfe appeared unconcerned, dropping down to use his saddle as a pillow and pulling his enormous hat over his eyes. Slocum thought the man slept but couldn't be sure.

"We have done well. Over twenty thousand pesos," she said after finishing her chore. "This will stand us in good stead."

"For what?" Slocum asked. "Why do we need the money if we're going to rob the mint?"

"Are all gringos so single-minded?" Belicia looked at Slocum coyly and batted her long eyelashes, then said in a whisper, "Of course, this is not so bad in *some* things." She turned slightly and the front of her white peasant blouse came unbuttoned, giving Slocum just a flash of firm brown breast.

"Aren't you going to divvy the take?" Slocum asked, still wondering about this side trip to rob a train.

"Divide it?" El Jéfe laughed. Slocum tried to keep from showing how jumpy he was. He hadn't known the bandido was standing so close to him. Slocum hoped El Jéfe hadn't heard the byplay with Belicia. He'd likely end up in a shallow grave or just left in the hot desert sun for the buzzards and ants.

"Your men risked their necks for the loot. Don't you give them their fair share?"

"Another *North Americano* tradition, eh? Fair? What is fair?" El Jéfe laughed as if this were the best joke he had ever heard.

"The money will be used for other things," Belicia said. Slocum saw how excited she was getting. He didn't know if it was the presence of so much money, him, El Jéfe, a combination of all that or something more. He couldn't begin to understand the thoughts flashing through her head. In some ways, this made her all the more desirable to him. It certainly made his position with the Estrada Gang increasingly dangerous.

"Mount. We ride once more!" El Jéfe rounded up his men, most of whom had taken only short naps and got them back into the saddle. They rode the rest of the day and stopped only when nightfall made riding hazardous. Before dawn the next morning they were again on the trail. By the time they reached Monterrey, Slocum was weaving in the saddle, more asleep than awake. The bandido leader pushed his men hard, and Slocum marveled at how well Belicia kept up. She never complained in spite of the fatigue and hunger. She rode as if she had a mission in Monterrey.

"There," El Jéfe said. "That is where we set up camp. See to it, Paco." He waved to his gargantuan assistant. "Belicia and I will go into Monterrey to speak with the guards." He laughed at this. The bandito leader waved to Belicia to mount. She waved to Slocum, then rode after the already galloping El Jéfe on his way to town.

Slocum wondered what he was expected to do. Paco went about his duty silently, pointing, grunting on occasion and once even cuffing a bandido who wasn't working hard enough. The site El Jéfe had chosen overlooked the city but gave scant view of the mint. Slocum wasn't sure why this particular spot appealed to the Mexican when others nearer the mint had been rejected.

He quickly discovered why.

Tents appeared as if by magic. Slocum walked around and found numerous caches already in place. The bandidos quickly turned the barren hillside into a small town using material stored for who knows how long. Paco continued to supervise, and Slocum saw nothing for him to do. He could pitch in, but this wasn't why Jim Hughes had sent him along. He edged away from the camp and found his horse. He got away without Paco noticing, rode downhill, then circled and headed into Monterrey to find what El Jéfe and Belicia were up to.

The town was richer than he remembered. He had ridden through a few years earlier when he had run with a gang of cattle rustlers working along the border. He'd make a quick trip into Texas, find a few hundred head and then bring them across the Rio Grande before the ranchers noticed—usually. One trip had been a disaster and he and a half dozen other rustlers had fallen into a trap. Slocum and three others had barely escaped with their lives, and the ranchers had hired bounty hunters to track down the rustlers. Slocum had reached Monterrey tired and not a little scared, still running hard to save his life, and kept on going when he hit the city.

Monterrey looked different to him now, like a plum waiting to be plucked. The vendors' stalls along the streets were loaded with produce, chickens and even a few pieces of stringy beef. The *peones* shopping in the marketplace had enough money to purchase such fine goods. And here and there in the crowd were *vaqueros* dressed with silver conchos and fancy duds and hand-tooled leather gunbelts that any man north of the border would kill for.

Slocum tried to stay as inconspicuous as possible in the crowd, though it was hard. People always noticed a gringo. He wasn't dressed as they were and carried a well-used six-shooter at his hip; mounted, he was a giant rivaling Paco. Knowing this attracted more attention than anything else, Slocum finally dismounted and walked his chestnut mare, preferring this slower, less visible mode of travel to riding and being noticed by everyone.

Through the crush Slocum noticed a tall, bobbing hat set with flashing pieces of silver. He turned in the direction of El Jéfe's huge hat and got as close as he could without being noticed. The bandido leader had changed his clothing and looked more than respectable; he looked downright prosperous. At his side stood a tall, gorgeous woman who might have ridden into town in style from the largest rancho in all Mexico. Slocum had to look twice before he decided that this was indeed Belicia Salazar.

She had been lovely before. Dressed up as she was, she was nothing less than magnificent.

She and El Jéfe dickered with an equally wealthy appearing man. They gestured and yelled at each other but there seemed to be no major disagreement. They bartered, and nothing more. In a few minutes, El Jéfe and the merchant shook hands, laughed, and threw their arms around each other. The merchant turned and bowed deeply to Belicia, then hurried off. El Jéfe spoke in a low voice to Belicia. Whatever he said, she agreed to quickly. She pulled up her mantilla and left.

Slocum was torn between following the woman and dogging El Jéfe's tracks. He chose the man, thinking he was likely to give some hint as to his plan to rob the mint.

Though the bandido walked slowly in the direction of the mint, he didn't go near it, staying too far away to inspect the defenses properly. Slocum wondered how long the outlaw had been planning this robbery. From the cache of tents on the hillside, it might be a plan of some standing.

El Jéfe went into one cantina after another, never staying for more than a sip of tequila or pulque before hurrying on. Such speed was uncharacteristic of the man and made Slocum wonder what was happening. Rather than try to keep up with him, Slocum stopped in one of the cantinas and sat for a drink.

He had to order in Spanish but didn't think the skill he betrayed would get back to El Jéfe. On the wall behind the bar was a small sign. Slocum slowly translated it as he drank his tequila.

"Interesting, eh?" asked the barkeep. "He salutes those who serve our country."

"*Soldados?*"

"Them," the barkeep agreed. "*Politicos*, also. Anyone with any power in Monterrey, he will give free drinks to this night."

"Who is he?"

The barkeep shrugged. "A veteran of many wars, he says. I think he is a *ladrino*."

"Why's that?"

Again Slocum got the eloquent shrug. "Who gives away liquor to soldiers? Diaz pays them well enough, but liquor? Pah! He would never do that for his own men. Why should this merchant do it for the Monterrey garrison?"

"All merchants are thieves, is that what you're saying?"

The barkeep laughed. "But of course. Why give away something that a dimwit could sell? Maybe he thinks to rob them with the cards. He spoke with one or two of the *soldados*." The barkeep pointed to a table in the rear of the cantina. Slocum picked up his shot glass and went to the rear.

"You will be at the merchant's camp tonight?" he asked. They looked up, surprised.

"Of course. We tell all our friends," said the younger of the two, a youth hardly eighteen.

"Not *all* our friends," said the older, wiser one of the pair. "We do not want them drinking all the tequila before we get our fill!"

"Gambling?" Slocum asked casually, seeing the cards spread between them.

"What else is there to do in this miserable city?" asked the younger soldier. "The women will have nothing to do with us."

Slocum didn't ask why. The reasons might have been as simple as not fraternizing with Diaz's cruel, repressive troops or the entire detachment might be from another province. There was still considerable clannish rivalry between states in Mexico that Diaz had never been able to extinguish through force of arms or the relative prosperity his long rule had brought.

"We will gamble till dawn," boasted the older soldier. "He promises us fine games."

"And women," the younger said. "There will be women for us. He said so, and he is an honorable man. One need only look at him to see this. So *rico*, so fine!"

"Good luck," Slocum said, seeing the kernel of El Jéfe's plan. The young troopers were bored, and the bandido offered them a night of free liquor and some excitement. It might take Hughes and the others a few more days to get the guano-laden burros into Monterrey. By that time, word would have spread about El Jéfe's generosity and every solider in the province would be coming around.

Including those guarding the mint.

Slocum left and wandered through the bustling city streets, finally passing by the mint. Four-story adobe walls surrounded the compound. A half dozen armed guards patrolled the area in front of the closed gates and on the battlements Slocum saw the heads of another

three guards. The gates were imposing—huge, timbered
portals that would take more than a single battering ram
to break through. The Mexican National Mint was not a
place to storm unless you had artillery and a hundred-man
company. It had to be taken by subterfuge.

El Jéfe might be the one to do it.

Slocum searched the streets for a sign of either the bandit
leader or Belicia, but didn't find them. He held back from
asking after them. Any number of people would have seen
or talked to them, but Slocum was leery of raising too much
of a ruckus. El Jéfe might hear. Spreading a few pesos
around Monterrey would insure him a good grapevine of
information.

Slocum mounted and rode slowly back up the hill over-
looking the city. Paco had finished setting up the tents, and
in a few of them Slocum saw cases of tequila and tables with
enough chairs around them for a major gambling parlor. He
didn't know what story El Jéfe had been passing out, but it
might just work after a few soldiers saw the vast quantities
of liquor available.

"Do you gamble, Señor Slocum?"

Again Slocum was startled by El Jéfe seeming to just
appear at his elbow. He hadn't heard the man walk over
and had no idea how long he had been watching him.

"Done a bit in my day."

"Honest gambling or have you learned a few tricks, eh?"
El Jéfe winked broadly.

"I can spot a cheat, if that's what you mean."

"No, not that. Can you cheat?"

Slocum dismounted and tied his horse to a low jacaranda
shrub, thinking hard about how to answer. He finally said,
"It depends on what you want me to do."

"You can deal from the bottom of a deck to win," El Jéfe
said obliquely, "or you can deal in such a way to lose. We
have no reason to win this night, do we?"

"Reckon not," Slocum said, getting the idea. Soldiers
who won would be more inclined to return, not only for

free liquor but for the pesos, also.

"Do you understand why the train needed to be robbed?" El Jéfe watched him closely, as if waiting for the proper reaction.

"That's the bankroll for all this, isn't it?"

"What else? I have learned what you gringos say so often. It takes money to make money. The first from the town will arrive soon. Get ready for them." El Jéfe thrust a thick wad of peso notes at him. Slocum riffled through the stack, seeing almost a thousand pesos. He tucked them into his vest pocket.

"There is another thing, Señor Slocum," said El Jéfe. "The six-shooter. Do not wear it. We are honest merchants traveling through Monterrey on our way to Mexico City. We have no need for such armament."

Slocum nodded. The soldiers would be less inclined to get their dander up if they saw only prosperous merchants willing to share their liquor and lose a few pesos gambling.

Slocum took his horse to the far side of the hill where Paco and two others had built a corral that afternoon. He put the mare inside and spent some time working on her, brushing her down and being sure she was fed before returning to the small city of tents. A few skeptical soldiers had wandered up from Monterrey, not sure what they would find. Slocum heard El Jéfe joking boisterously with them, promising them an evening of entertainment because he appreciated their devotion to duty, their loyalty, their sacrifice for the people of Mexico. If the bandido laid on the compliments too thick, none of the soldiers seemed to notice. As with the two Slocum had met, these were young men, almost boys, and too naive to be skeptical for long.

When Slocum saw Belicia whirling through the small crowd, he knew not one of the soldiers would be leaving any time soon. She almost danced as she flitted from one to another, whispering in one's ear, laughing and then rushing on before he became too amorous. Slocum didn't have to hear what she was saying to know the lure.

He heaved a deep breath and pushed back a canvas covering the entrance to one of the tents. Inside, a large table had already been set with bottles of tequila, glasses, and a deck of cards. Slocum waited until three youthful *soldados* came in. He held up the deck and asked, "Anyone interested?"

They didn't speak English but the sight of the cards being fanned out on the table was translation enough. Slocum began playing, at first for the penny ante stakes set by the impoverished soldiers. Then, as they won more and more of the thousand peso roll El Jéfe had given him for this purpose, their bets became wilder and their drinking heavier. They enjoyed themselves and laughed raucously. The more the lonely men joked and drank, the wilder their betting became. And still Slocum lost. It took until after three in the morning for him to toss in his last crumpled bill.

Never had he stacked the deck more, dealt from the bottom faster or been quicker to fold with a winning hand. He had lost hands that would have made him well-to-do, but not as rich as five hundred pounds of silver from the Monterrey mint. That thought came back to him every time he saw a young soldier make a foolish bet, draw to an inside straight or even bluff with a pair of deuces. A few pesos now traded for a quarter ton of precious metal.

Rich for the rest of his life. Slocum could afford to lose money that wasn't even his to keep that dream alive.

He pushed into the night and sucked in a lungful of damp breeze blowing off the distant water. This felt better than the intense heat of the Sonora Desert, but he knew he wouldn't be long in this town. They would have to ride like the wind to get out of Monterrey after stealing all the mint had to offer.

Most of the soldiers had drunk themselves into a stupor. A few had friends to help them back to barracks in town. Others curled up under bushes and trees and slept like babies. El Jéfe had delivered on the promises of tequila and gambling. Slocum wondered if Belicia had delivered on the promises she had made.

He heard her voice drifting on the wind and turned toward it. She and El Jéfe stood shoulder to shoulder, but only for a moment. He took her in his arms and kissed her. Slocum stiffened, his hand drifting toward his left hip, but he had put his Colt Navy into his bedroll. The bandido and Belicia went into a tent and the light winked out. Slocum stood and watched for several minutes, listening to the sound of their voices.

Knowing he was only torturing himself, Slocum left the camp to bed down for the night. But sleep was long in coming. Belicia's joyous laughter continued to haunt him and keep sleep at bay.

6

Slocum awoke a little before dawn from a fitful, dream-racked sleep. He couldn't get the nightmarish image of Belicia going into El Jéfe's tent from his mind. She might not consider him anything more than a moment's diversion. He had come across her when she was bathing, and she had let him make love to her. For Belicia this might be nothing.

For Slocum it had turned into more. He knew he was wrong becoming so enamored of her. He might end up being dead wrong. She was El Jéfe's woman. Or was she? So much of the relationship between Belicia Salazar and El Jéfe was hidden from him that Slocum didn't know what to believe. The two hardly spoke to each other for almost a week, then they went off and spent the night together in the bandido's tent. It didn't make any sense to him, and he might be reading more into their single quick lovemaking than was there.

Slocum knew better than to think with his balls, but he was doing it all the same.

"A quarter ton of silver. My cut of the robbery," he said to himself. "Balance that against Belicia's favors. Five hundred pounds of silver." Being rich was nice. He could buy all the women he wanted.

None would be as beautiful or enticing as Belicia, though.

He pushed himself to a sitting position and studied the sky. He had almost an hour before the sun rose. Those in the bandido camp might sleep far later because of the revelry the night before. Slocum's head felt like a rotten melon ready to explode; he'd drunk too much tequila, but he had to get up. Hughes was depending on him, and he still worried that El Jéfe might be planning a double-cross. Everybody could get rich if they pulled off the robbery.

Without the gringos taking a cut, all the bandidos could be fabulously rich.

Slocum strapped on his cross-draw holster and settled the Colt on his hip. He had missed the hogleg last night. The *soldados* carried their carbines and sidearms. He had felt naked. Slocum smiled wryly. Maybe it had been for the best. The few who had spoken broken English had quizzed him about being with El Jéfe since he was obviously not a *rico* merchant. Slocum had been forced to use his brains rather than his six-shooter to convince them he was all right.

The liquor had also helped, he knew, and if he had ever won a big hand there might have been hell to pay. But the soldiers weren't likely to ask too many questions when their dry-as-a-desert thirst was being slaked for free and they were winning. And for all they knew there might have been women in the camp.

Belicia. He shuddered at the thought of the woman whoring, even to get them inside the mint without a fight.

Slocum rolled his blanket and stuffed it under a convenient bush. Then he walked past the sleeping guard at the corral, saddled his mare and walked her downhill until he thought it was safe to mount. No one stirred in El Jéfe's camp. Such carelessness on the eve of the big robbery wasn't good, but Slocum wasn't complaining.

He rode through the dark-shrouded streets of the city until he came to the imposing walls around the mint. Two guards slept at the gate, their heads resting on their raised knees. Their carbines were stacked between them for easy grabbing, should the need arise. Slocum wanted to be sure it didn't.

He left his horse in an alley and walked slowly around the fortress that was the Mexican National Mint. It confirmed his reconnaissance of the day before. A small army would be needed to get in without laying siege to the place. The rattle of a supply wagon caught his attention. It passed within a few feet. Slocum shouldn't have done it, but he reacted rather than thought. He took three quick steps, broke into a run and caught up with the wagon. Chains dangled under the heavily laden wagon bed. He grabbed one and pulled hard, twisting as the wagon jerked him off his feet.

Kicking hard, he lifted himself up to the rude bed of chains and hung there, the iron links cutting into his flesh. The wagon slowed and the driver hailed the sleeping guards. They recognized the man and waved him through the gate. Slocum hung precariously, hoping the still sleepy *soldados* wouldn't examine the wagon.

He need not have worried. They were asleep before the gate swung open and the wagon rattled through. He dropped off just inside the gate and rolled, landing in a heap of garbage. He lay still, waiting to hear if a cry went up.

After almost a minute, no one rallied the garrison to arms to repel the one-man invasion. Glad to be able to move from the stinking pile of refuse, Slocum pushed up on his arms and looked around like a lizard on a hot rock. Much of the interior courtyard was hidden in shadow, but he saw enough to know that he had chosen a good time to make his incursion. The few guards wandering about looked as if they had just awakened. None paid any attention as Slocum stood and walked slowly toward the thick adobe wall guarding the compound.

Back against the cool adobe, he began sidling along the wall, mentally noting every guard's position and where the central buildings most likely to hold the silver were. He didn't like what he saw. Gun placements covered every entrance to the largest of the buildings. To pry loose even a single soldier from his protected point would require more than dynamite. If they had to fight they'd need a Gatling gun or a small cannon.

Getting either weapon through the main gate would require more than just knocking or sneaking in as he had done. By the time they'd fought inside to use a cannon, the word would have gone out to other posts. In no time the entire town of Monterrey would be crawling with *Federales* intent on stopping the theft from their mint.

Slocum saw the first fingers of a pearly dawn glowing over the tall walls and knew he didn't have much time. He chose a bold course. He straightened his back and marched directly for the building where the coins must be minted. He hadn't gotten ten paces when a guard challenged him.

"¡*Estúpido!*" he shouted back. "*Estoy el comandante.*" He didn't wait to see if claiming to be the garrison commander worked. He spun in a military right face and marched away from the building. For what seemed an eternity he waited for the bullet to blast apart his spine. It never came. He came to a halt, bent over, then dived for cover behind the pile of garbage that had sheltered him when he'd entered the mint. His heart thumped wildly. He knew how close he had come to being discovered, and he still had to get out of the compound with his hide in one piece.

Once again, luck came his way. A small wagon rattled to a halt beside the garbage heap. A hunched-over man got down from the box, pain echoing from his every movement. He grabbed a shovel and began scooping the garbage into the back of his wagon. Slocum knew he'd never have a better chance. He rose up and said quietly, "*Ayudo.*"

He began shoveling the garbage in with his hands. In a few seconds he was so filthy no one could tell without a close inspection that he was a gringo. The garbage man stared at him for a moment, shrugged and handed him the shovel. Slocum took it, wondering what was happening. The man motioned for him to continue working. Slocum did so with as much speed as he could muster.

When the wagon was loaded and the garbage pile reduced to a small smear, the man took the shovel back and tossed it into the bed. He stared at Slocum for a moment, as if wondering what might happen. Slocum climbed into the wagon, settling down in the smelly refuse. The man groaned and got into the box, flicked the reins and got the swaybacked mule moving. The gate guard waved them through without even looking in the back. Before the man had rattled more than a hundred yards down the street, Slocum jumped out, leaving behind a trail of offal. He shook himself like a wet dog and got most of it off, but the odor lingered.

He looked around until he found a simple fountain. Women were beginning to fill buckets from it, but Slocum didn't even look at them. He took off his Colt and plunged into the shallow fountain. The warm water engulfed him and rinsed some of the stench from his clothes. He got out and brushed off more of the garbage. Then he wrung out his shirt the best he could. It wasn't a proper bath but it would have to do. The sun was coming up, and he knew El Jéfe would miss him if he didn't get back into camp soon.

The brief trip into the compound had convinced him that El Jéfe would never rob the mint like he had the train. The plan of using the burros and the Hughes Bunch as backup looked more feasible with every detail Slocum found out, but he was already missing Jim Hughes and the others. He needed someone to watch his back. Slocum felt as if he had been caught in the jaws of a vise tightening down around him.

He put his horse into the corral, aware that Paco was watching intently. The huge Mexican couldn't ask where he had been, but Slocum knew the word had been passed to El Jéfe that the gringo had been out of camp. By the time he climbed the rise to the small city of tents, El Jéfe was ready for him.

The bandido had a chair stationed outside his tent, a king's throne waiting for the royal audience to begin. Slocum swallowed bile when he remembered this was the tent El Jéfe and Belicia had gone into the night before. The laughter that had come from inside then still haunted him. He put on his best poker face as he walked past the outlaw.

"Ah, Señor Slocum, you are ready for the next part of our scheme." El Jéfe stopped speaking and wrinkled his nose. He started to say something, bit it back, then finally asked, "Where have you spent the night? In a compost heap?"

"Been doing some looking around," Slocum said. "Your plan to get into the mint is a good one."

"You have been inside the compound?" El Jéfe's eyebrows rose. "That is dangerous. You accused me of foolishness robbing the train. The money was needed for all you see. But to enter the mint. No." He shook his head violently. "This is wrong."

"I wanted to check it out for myself."

"Any disturbance now will ruin all we work for." El Jéfe fingered the silver-filigreed handle of the .44 he had stuck into a broad hand-tooled leather belt.

"No one saw me," Slocum said. "I need to take a bath."

"There is water . . . and a tub," El Jéfe said. Slocum fought to keep his face from showing any emotion. Had Belicia told him about making love to Slocum in the bath tub? Or had he guessed? Was he shooting in the dark to find out? Slocum didn't know how subtle El Jéfe could be. It might have been an innocent enough comment, although Slocum doubted anything the bandido did was entirely innocent.

"Thanks. I need to get the smell washed off. Don't want to scare the soldiers off tonight."

"No, no we do not want that," El Jéfe said. He hiked one knee over the arm of his chair and gazed down into

Monterrey, pointedly ignoring Slocum. Dismissed, Slocum scrounged around camp until he found the tub El Jéfe had set up for his men. Few availed themselves of it, Slocum saw. There was hardly any disturbance in the dust and mud around the tub. That was fine with Slocum. He needed to soak and give his clothing a thorough washing. As much as he wanted to linger, though, he didn't. He had to be sure El Jéfe wasn't going to simply gun him down to eliminate an annoyance.

Slocum washed quickly, got his clothes as clean as possible and let them dry in the hot summer sun. It took less than twenty minutes from the time he'd stepped into the tub until he was snaking his way back up the hill behind El Jéfe's tent. Inside the bandido spoke rapidly, probably with Paco since there was no response to anything he said.

Pulling up the bottom flap of the tent, Slocum peered in. He was right. Paco stood solemnly in front of his leader nodding now and then but mostly taking the torrent of abuse without any show of emotion. Though it was entirely in Spanish, Slocum caught most of it. El Jéfe was dressing Paco down for letting the gringo sneak into town. Slocum tensed when El Jéfe ordered Paco to kill him with bare hands if he tried again. Slocum touched the Colt Navy at his hip. Paco was big, but a round or two from the trusty six-shooter would bring him down.

El Jéfe went on but nothing concerned Slocum. He started to slip away when he heard Hughes mentioned. He tried to catch what El Jéfe was saying but two of the bandidos came up and Slocum had to get away fast. He slid down the hill, getting dirty again and not caring. He circled the hill and came up the front way, as if he had just finished bathing. El Jéfe had left his tent again and watched Slocum.

"You need another bath," El Jéfe said. "Already you are dirty, even if you smell less ripe."

"I'll be ready for this evening. What's there to do till then? Any word from Hughes?" Slocum added the last to see the bandido's reaction. He decided he wouldn't want to play poker with this man. There wasn't a flicker of emotion on El Jéfe's face.

"There is nothing to do. And of Señor Hughes? There is nothing to report. We begin early this night. There will be far more *soldados* than before." El Jéfe laughed and went off, Paco a step behind him. The huge man's eyes followed Slocum until they vanished in the direction of the corral. It was all Slocum could do to keep from drawing his Colt and putting a bullet in the man's head. That would eliminate one source of danger, and it'd bring the Hughes Bunch–Estrada Gang alliance tumbling down.

Five hundred pounds of silver. It echoed in Slocum's head and held him tighter than any jail cell.

Slocum spent the day chewing on grass and staring into the distance, wondering if Hughes was anywhere near. They'd been separated over a week now. The Hughes Bunch should have stolen the burros without any trouble and then made their way into Mexico. Slocum was getting antsy and wanted the robbery done with. He didn't have any proof El Jéfe was planning a double-cross, but it seemed likely and he had to talk with Hughes.

And where was Belicia? Slocum hadn't seen her all day. He lay back and watched thin white clouds scud across the sky. He thought hard about the woman and what he felt for her. Somewhere along the way, Slocum drifted off to sleep, only to be awakened by loud laughter. He sat bolt upright and peered down the hill. A driver recklessly tried to bring a loaded wagon straight up to the top of the hill—a wagon filled with pushing, joking women. From the coarseness of their talk Slocum knew someone had been recruiting whores in Monterrey.

Somehow he wasn't as surprised as he was disappointed when he saw Belicia with them. She had been busy finding this many loose women to entertain the soldiers. As the wagon rolled by, Belicia blew him a kiss. Slocum didn't move a muscle until the wagon passed him. Belicia laughed, either at his lack of response or at some crude joke about gringos being told by another woman in the wagon.

Slocum walked slowly up the hill. A dozen or more soldiers had already gathered for the free liquor. When they saw the women, they went wild. It took some doing for El Jéfe to keep them apart. Somehow he did it without starting any serious fights.

"They are for later, *mis amigos*," El Jéfe promised. "Enjoy their company now, let them give you tequila, let them bring you luck as you gamble. And later you will be lucky, eh?" He laughed and the soldiers believed every word of it.

Slocum avoided Belicia and went into the tent he had occupied the night before. Six soldiers crowded the table, waiting to fleece the *Norteamericano* with the bad luck at cards. Slocum started to back out when El Jéfe entered. Slocum felt another wad of pesos thrust into his hand, his stake for the evening.

"Enjoy, my friends, enjoy gambling. I am repaying you for all you have done for me during my years as merchant. Drink, eh? Here, Luisa and Consuela and María will serve you. They *like* soldiers." El Jéfe winked broadly to Slocum, then left to attend to the men and politicians from Monterrey in other tents. Slocum settled down for another night of losing slowly to the soldiers, and he did.

It took longer for him to lose the money this night, though, because so many left the game early to go with the whores. Up and down the hill he heard women urging their men on and men laughing with delight at having a woman once more.

Slocum tried to keep his mind off what Belicia might be doing for the cause of robbing the mint. It turned his stomach but he kept dealing and losing.

After four in the morning he left the tent, tired, slightly drunk and ready to fall asleep. Slocum stopped and stared when he saw Belicia standing under a tree. Many women came and went, but always Belicia stayed by the tree as if directing the trollops but never joining in their activities. Some hope rose inside Slocum that she hadn't been with any of the soldiers. He started to go to her when two of El Jéfe's men walked past, talking in low voices.

They spoke in rapid Spanish. One glanced in his direction but neither gave any sign that they knew he understood what they said. Slocum's heart sped when he heard one say, "Tomorrow, if the gringos come with the burros."

The other replied, "Then, we get them inside." Both laughed at this. El Jéfe did plan a double-cross and it was going to be done inside the mint.

Slocum continued walking toward the tree where Belicia had been, but the woman had vanished in the night like some ghost. He looked back at El Jéfe's tent and heard laughter from inside. Slocum's heart turned cold and rock-hard. It seemed as if the silver would be all he'd get out of this—if he could keep the Mexicans from double-crossing the Hughes Bunch.

7

Slocum didn't like waiting. Usually, he was as patient as any man alive but he had to reach Hughes and let him know all he had discovered. Not only had he heard two of El Jéfe's men discussing what had to be a double-cross, he had pumped a young corporal for information about the interior of the mint and had discovered another obstacle to be overcome. Just getting past a minimal patrol of guards was the least of their worries. Once inside the compound, the silver used to mint the Mexican coins was kept in a massive vault.

The corporal didn't know which of the men inside the garrison knew the combination. Two officers might, the young soldier had decided after much drunken rumination, but he was not sure which two. Slocum hadn't been able to continue pumping him for information; a whore had come by and singled out the handsome corporal. He went off all too willingly and Slocum didn't see him again that night.

Slocum hadn't been told of El Jéfe's plans after they were inside the mint, but he was able to guess. Paco and the others would come roaring up after taking care of the soldiers in the tent city and trap the Hughes Bunch. A few quick shots and that would be it. The Estrada Gang would leave with the silver-laden burros and lose themselves in the vast reaches of the Sierra Madres.

And Belicia. What had become of her? Slocum had sought her in camp but had met only stony silence when he'd asked after her. She had gone into Monterrey, of that he was sure, but to do what? Recruit more whores for the night's festivities? He alternated between thinking she was hardly better than any of the women she had supplied for the soldiers' pleasure and a more lenient guess that she was only doing her part for the robbery.

"Señor Slocum, there you are. Why do you pace like the caged animal?" El Jéfe walked up. Paco followed a pace behind his leader, a mountain of a man waiting to crush Slocum. He balled his huge hands into fists and squeezed so hard his bones cracked. The way he stared at Slocum showed he wanted the gringo's head under those powerful fingers.

"I'm getting tired of waiting. What do you hear from Hughes?"

"We will soon be moving toward riches," El Jéfe assured him. "We have not been idle. Nor has your leader, the estimable Señor Hughes."

Slocum stared at the bandido. He didn't speak like any simple peasant rising up from poverty to take his share. Then again, Belicia was no peasant. The look of her hands showed her to be fresh off the ranch, pampered and never having missed a meal in her life. But she had a hard edge to her that didn't set with this appraisal. It had been a spell since she'd been waited on hand and foot.

And El Jéfe was as much a mystery for Slocum.

"When do we go for the silver?"

"So much impatience. Señor Slocum, I have worked for years to be sure this is just so. There must be no, what do you call it, buck fever to rob me of my riches. This is the robbery of a lifetime."

Slocum considered what he had heard the two bandidos saying as they passed by, not knowing he understood their conversation. He couldn't keep from asking obliquely. "What happens when we get inside the compound?"

"That is the most important part," El Jéfe said, his face neutral. Slocum had expected some small flicker of surprise, of deceit, of some emotion. El Jéfe betrayed nothing. He began worrying that El Jéfe's own men might be planning the double-cross, dealing out their leader as well as the gringos. Slocum almost broached this to him when Belicia came riding up. Slocum knew he'd lost El Jéfe's attention, no matter what he might say because the bandido turned and went toward the lovely woman, his hands outstretched.

"So good to see you, *bella mía*," El Jéfe cried. Belicia smiled brightly and hit the ground before the horse had come to a complete halt. El Jéfe caught her in his arms and spun her around. Slocum stood and watched, his insides cold and hollow.

"All is ready. I spoke with one of them, the one with sandy hair," Belicia said. "They will arrive by mid-afternoon."

"Perfect," El Jéfe said, rubbing his hands together. This was the most emotion Slocum had seen the bandido display in some time. He walked over and stood a few paces away. El Jéfe turned to him and smiled crookedly.

"Belicia met with one of your leader's men."

"The one named Doc Neal," she said. "He is young but seems able to handle himself well."

"He's a good man," Slocum said, remembering how Doc Neal had frozen up and hadn't fired when he should have. The entire payroll robbery had been a fiasco and he couldn't much fault the youngster for getting confused. He just hoped Doc Neal had gotten over not being able to use his rifle when bullets started flying. Once inside the mint, they'd need every gun they had.

"They want me to join them?" Slocum asked.

"He said nothing of this. They are a few miles outside Monterrey now, with fully thirty burros loaded with guano. Doc Neal is arranging with the dealer across the plaza from the mint to take delivery of the guano. The price is absurdly low and everyone buzzes about how the merchant has taken the gringos." Belicia laughed. "This could not be better. No one will want to be near to watch the transaction for fear of laughing. The merchant would skin them alive in such a case."

"But after," El Jéfe said, enjoying this immensely, "after the gringos have unloaded their guano, he will boast for months."

"Even when he finds out he's been used?" Slocum asked.

"That makes the jest all the richer," El Jéfe said. "I must speak with the others and prepare for this evening. Nothing must go wrong."

Belicia hesitated, her eyes locking with Slocum's. He wasn't sure what he read there. She was eager for everything to be moving, just as he was. That was apparent, but there was something more than he didn't recognize. It was an almost religious fervor.

"All will go well, John. And soon we can . . . talk at greater length."

Before he could reply, El Jéfe called to her. She reached out and touched him on the cheek, then hurried off. Slocum stood and stared down at Monterrey, wondering what the hell was going on. This was the robbery of a lifetime, and he wasn't even sure if the people he relied on were going to double-cross him. What were Belicia's motives? The more he saw of her, the less he thought she wanted silver from the mint.

That wasn't true of El Jéfe. But were the bandido leader's men plotting to shoot him in the back? Or had Slocum completely misunderstood what he had overheard? The two might have been commenting on teaming up with the Hughes Bunch and working to get them inside the mint where they could steal the silver and load the burros for the getaway. There might not have been a double-cross intended, but Slocum had read it into their words because he was looking for it.

Jim Hughes had poisoned him, telling him the Mexicans might be ready to cross them. He had sought it and had found it.

" 'The wicked flee when no man pursues,' " Slocum quoted. "And you're always bound to find crooks if you look hard enough for them."

He didn't know what to do. The soldiers wouldn't begin drifting up the hill from the town for quite a few hours yet. The cases of tequila were being readied and the whores would be arriving soon, just for *Los Bandidos de la Estrada*. El Jéfe knew how to keep his men happy and ready for the night. Slocum wasn't sure what they would do to hogtie the soldiers, but if they got them drunk enough and engrossed in winning, not to mention all the women they could want, the young men might never want to leave the camp no matter what went on in town.

He wandered the camp aimlessly until almost twilight and the first of the soldiers began arriving. Hughes and the others ought to be in town across from the mint, selling their bat shit and getting the burros ready for real loads. Slocum made a quick decision. He had to talk to Hughes and warn him of possible danger inside from the bandidos. He saw Belicia and El Jéfe walking arm in arm from one tent to the next. This decided for him. There was nothing for him here; his lot was cast with the Hughes Bunch.

Slocum made his way to the corral and found it unguarded. Paco and the others were on top of the hill getting ready for the rush of soldiers. With any luck, some guards might abandon their posts to partake of the whores and booze since El Jéfe had made it clear that this would be the last night the "merchants" would be camped outside Monterrey. Every man would want to partake of the free carnal delights one last time.

He rode quickly into town, not wanting to tire his chestnut mare unduly but needing to make good time to meet Hughes before they positioned themselves. Slocum wasn't sure if he would be missed in camp. The soldiers wouldn't come to gamble. They had done well the two prior nights. This night would be reserved for more basic needs like liquor and women.

But El Jéfe would notice. Nothing escaped that man's sharp eyes.

Slocum went directly to the plaza. Many of the town's merchants were closing shop for the day and a steady stream of soldiers from the garrison wended its way through the streets like a column of ants headed for a summer's picnic. The draw of free liquor and women worked well.

Slocum found the long line of burros waiting to be unloaded at precisely the spot he thought. Sandy King and Zwing Hunt lounged nearby, their feet up and a bottle of tequila sitting between them. Hunt nudged his friend when he saw Slocum. They whispered to each other, obviously arguing over whether to show any recognition.

Not having time to do much more than nod in their direction, Slocum hurried past, not caring what decision they reached. Jim Hughes couldn't be too far off. Slocum peered into the dim adobe hut the guano merchant called his store and saw Curly Bill and Hughes.

He hit the ground and whirled the reins around a convenient post, hardly breaking stride as he did so. Slocum got to the door and called out, "Hughes, got to talk with you. Let Bill handle the rest of the dealings."

"Slocum?" The outlaw was startled at Slocum's sudden intrusion. "Can't it wait?" Hughes wanted to maintain the fiction of being a traveling guano merchant awhile longer. Slocum wouldn't have argued if he had been sure of El Jéfe's intentions.

"Got to talk *now*."

Hughes signaled Curly Bill to finish off, getting as much as they could for their cargo, as if it mattered. He went to the door, looked up and down the street and then muttered in a low voice, "This is stupid, Slocum. They might see us talking."

"The guards from the mint are all on their way up to the tents," Slocum said. "They don't count. This is about El Jéfe."

"I knew it," grated Hughes. "The son of a bitch is going to double-cross us!"

"Don't know that for a fact, but you've got to be on guard once you get inside the walls. I heard two of them talking and it sounded like they were—" Slocum bit off his words when he heard gunfire from outside town. The reports were distant, faint but unmistakable; one shot followed another and another and still another until it sounded as if a war was being fought.

"Get moving, Hughes, get a move on!" came the cry from down the street. Doc Neal waved his hat wildly and motioned them to action. "They done started killin' the lot 'em up on the hill. We got to do it now!"

"Son of a bitch," Hughes swore again. "Let's get it over with. And thanks, Slocum, we'll be watching our backs. You take that rifle of yours and guard the rear. We're gonna be rich tonight if we have to kill every last one of them Mexican bastards!"

Slocum saw Doc Neal's cry had alerted Hunt and King. Both men leaped to their feet, knocking over the tequila bottle. Neither noticed in his haste to pull out his six-shooters. Curly Bill erupted from the store, his pistol clutched in his hand. He looked around, a wild glint in his eye. He tore off across the plaza, heading straight for the gate leading into the mint. Slocum wasn't sure this was the best way of attacking the garrison since there must be soldiers left inside, but the frontal assault took the few remaining soldiers by surprise. One even opened the gate to see what the commotion was.

Curly Bill leveled his six-shooter and shot the man square in the middle of his face, then kept running, using the fallen body as a steppingstone to get into the grounds of the mint. Hunt and King got the burros moving and Jim Hughes joined Curly Bill a few seconds later. Doc Neal came riding up, his eyes wide.

"What happened?" Slocum called to him. "What's going on up on the hill?"

"They're cutting 'em all down. They just opened fire and are slaughterin' the lot of 'em." Fear was etched on the young man's face.

"Who? The soldiers are killing—"

"No, no, the Estrada Gang's killing the drunk soldiers. Just murdering them. No quarter."

"*Deguello*," muttered Slocum. No quarter given.

"What are we going to do?" Doc Neal cried.

"Rob the damned mint, that's what," Slocum said. If El Jéfe was busy slaughtering the soldiers, it would take a few minutes before he and his men could turn their attention to the mint. Slocum told Doc Neal to stand guard outside, not wanting the frightened man with him if gunplay was necessary.

Slocum found that Curly Bill and Jim Hughes had already done most of the work. El Jéfe had emptied the compound of most of the guards. The three or four remaining had fallen easy prey to the deadly fire from Curly Bill's six-gun. Hughes had done little more than finish off one of the badly wounded soldiers Bill had left behind.

"We've got to get into that building," Slocum said, pointing out the central structure. "The doors might still be open."

Curly Bill kicked open the tall doors and burst in, gun blazing. Slocum wasn't sure if anyone was even inside, but this time he favored the other outlaw's approach. There wasn't time to waste getting bogged down in a gunfight. Slocum and Hughes followed closely on Curly Bill's heels and found the huge room empty. To one side loomed minting machines for punching out coins. A small foundry melted the silver, and bags of coins lined one wall.

"This is it!" cried Curly Bill. "We found the Promised Land!"

"No, don't bother with those," Hughes said. "In the vault. Get into the vault." He pointed to a pair of immense steel doors. Slocum saw that getting through them would take a dozen sticks of dynamite.

"King and Hunt can get the bags of coins loaded on one burro," he told Hughes, "but we aren't getting in there easily."

"Yeah, you think so?" Hughes waved and King dragged out a crate of dynamite. "You fix a fuse? With a twenty-second delay?"

Slocum grabbed the roll of black miner's fuse and measured off six inches. That gave them half a minute to get out before the entire crate of dynamite went off. He bit down on the blasting cap and crimped the fuse, then thrust it into the middle of the crate. He fumbled in his pocket for a lucifer, struck it, and applied the smoking end to the black fuse. It sputtered and let out a hiss, filling his eyes with choking smoke. Slocum backed off, then ran. He yelled "Fire in the hole!" and dived through the door just after King wrestled out the last bag of silver coins. The explosion rocked the mint to its foundations.

Slocum brushed the burning debris off his shirt and scrambled to his feet. Through the dust and smoke he saw a sight that made his jaw drop. Slocum hadn't thought anything could give him such a feeling of surprise and even awe.

He was wrong. Dead wrong. He stared into the open vault and saw row after row of silver bars and canvas bags so loaded with silver coins the seams threatened to split.

"Ain't it about the most beautiful sight you ever saw?" whispered Jim Hughes.

"Let's get it loaded, then talk about it," Slocum said, still worrying about soldiers and the Estrada Gang. They formed a bucket brigade, one in the vault tossing a bag to the next and the next until the sack arrived outside to be loaded onto a burro. Slocum's arms were turning to lead from the heavy weight of silver passing through his hands. His back felt as if it might snap at any instant from the load. But nothing could stop him. Every ache and pain was pure ecstasy. He had hoped there might be thousands of dollars of silver in the Monterrey Mint waiting for them. There had to be at least a million, more money than Slocum had ever even imagined.

"How are we doing?" Hughes called out. "How many animals you got loaded?"

"A dozen, Jim, we got a dozen loaded," Hunt called. "And we got that many more to go. God, we're fucking rich, rich!" Zwing Hunt cackled like a hen, and Slocum didn't mind in the least. He felt like crying for joy himself.

Until he turned to pass a sack laden with silver coins to Sandy King. Standing in the doorway, hands on his hips, was El Jéfe. Paco loomed behind him and through the gathering gloom outside Slocum made out the rest of the Estrada Gang.

Doc Neal hadn't given them warning, and now they were trapped inside at the mercy of El Jéfe. Slocum knew the bandido's long suit wasn't benevolence.

8

Slocum reached for his Colt but knew he'd never be able to shoot fast enough. The Mexicans had them boxed in and could gun them down with no trouble.

The expected fusillade never came. El Jéfe walked through the smoke and dust like a conquering hero. He waved to include all of them when he said, "*Bueno*, this is very good. You have done well, my friends. My men will help you load the burros for the getaway."

Slocum started to speak but no words came. He might have misunderstood the barely overheard conversation back in the camp. The two bandidos might have only been talking about getting the Hughes Bunch inside the mint for the robbery rather than maneuvering the gringos into a vulnerable position to kill them. He didn't know. Slocum started to mention the incident but a ruckus outside took both Hughes and El Jéfe away in a rush.

Sporadic but well-directed gunfire had begun to turn the compound into a deadly arena. Zwing Hunt had been hit and was clutching his leg, cursing a blue streak. Sandy King stood by him, firing wildly in the direction of the partially open gate. "Goddamn soldiers are coming in. They didn't get all of 'em!"

Slocum saw that they would be bottled up good and proper unless they fought hard now. He shouted to Curly Bill, thinking he was most likely to do what had to be done.

"Attack! Straight down their throats!"

He hung back and waited for the other man to begin the suicidal rush. To his surprise it worked and Curly Bill didn't get ventilated. Gunfire behind the soldiers caught them in a lethal crossfire. Doc Neal had finally gotten over his fright and came to their aid. His shooting wasn't too accurate, but Slocum didn't mind that. It kept the soldiers occupied while he started his own deadly fire. He killed two and wounded a third. Slocum wasn't sure how many Curly Bill killed, first with his six-gun and then when it came up empty, with his bare hands. The man had turned into a killing machine that completely routed the frightened soldiers.

"Get those burros loaded," Hughes called to Hunt and King. Paco began lugging four bags of silver coins at a time from the blasted vault and halved the time it took to get the remaining pack animals loaded down with enough wealth for a small country.

"Will it be enough for you, Señor Slocum?"

Slocum turned to El Jéfe, who grinned broadly. The bandido looked demonic with a smear of black running diagonally across his cheek and a thin cut turning bloody on his forehead.

"It's a start," Slocum said, wondering if the double-cross would come. He was still suspicious of the Mexicans.

"Get the pack train moving to the mountains. We will cover your trail. Hughes knows where we are to rendezvous." El Jéfe paused for a moment, then smiled even more broadly. "It has been a pleasure." He thrust out his hand. Slocum hesitated for a moment, then shook it. He wasn't sure he could ever really like this man, but he had to respect him for his bravery and audacity planning this robbery.

Slocum waved to King and Hunt to get the burros moving. He didn't know where they were headed but out of Monterrey was the best bet. The sudden appearance of soldiers when he'd thought El Jéfe had taken care of them warned Slocum of worse things to come.

He mounted and rode to the gate. Curly Bill stood with his feet spread wide, his six-gun waving around in wild circles as he hunted for something more to kill. Doc Neal had ridden to the far side of the plaza and waved to them. Slocum was barely able to see the man through the gloom, but that was fine with him. If he couldn't see Neal, neither could the authorities, if any were still alive. He had thought El Jéfe would just keep the soldiers occupied with liquor and women, but the gunfire had convinced him the bandido had murdered the lot of them.

Standing in his stirrups, Slocum took a quick look around, hoping to see Belicia. Either she had already ridden on or hadn't accompanied El Jéfe. The burros began grumbling as they passed Slocum, some weighted down so much their legs bowed slightly, but the valiant little animals carried more than a mule and weren't as difficult to handle. Slocum saw each burro had either eight or ten sacks of coin slung over its back. There were at least two hundred fifty pounds of silver on each animal.

Slocum's quick mind worked that out to over six hundred pounds of silver for each man taking part in the robbery, maybe as much as seven hundred. He sank back into his saddle and worked through the numbers. Not believing them, he did it again. He kept coming up with his cut amounting to as much as fifty thousand dollars. That would make him more than rich. He'd be fabulously wealthy, considering his father seldom saw more than a hundred dollars cash money in a year of farming.

The burros fell into a rhythm as they wended their way through the twisting streets. They could maintain this pace all night, if necessary, and Slocum thought it might be. Hughes and Curly Bill mounted and were joining Hunt and

King. Doc Neal rode ahead to scout the way. And Slocum should have been on his way to get the hell out of town with them, but something still didn't sit right with him.

"Go on," he called to Hughes. "I'll catch up."

"What's wrong?"

Slocum shook his head. He couldn't put it into words. He had been wrong about El Jéfe's men double-crossing them inside the mint. Maybe they intended on letting the Hughes Bunch get the silver out of Monterrey before ambushing them. But he hadn't read any duplicity in El Jéfe's congratulation. The Mexican had seemed sincere. El Jéfe's emotions were always under control, but Slocum thought he knew genuine sentiment from fake. The bandido wasn't planning to cross them.

"Where's El Jéfe?"

"Who cares?" called back Hughes. "If he doesn't show up, it's *all* ours."

"There must be something else," Slocum said, more to himself than to Hughes. That was the only reason El Jéfe wasn't riding with the silver. He had a few men riding with the Hughes Bunch, but they'd be no good if Hughes turned on them. El Jéfe wasn't stupid and yet he was letting the take from the robbery slip through his hands. There *had* to be something more.

And Belicia? Where was she? Earlier she had been excited at the prospect of the robbery. Even if she didn't take direct part, she was involved. Why not stick around and watch, unless something more important drew her away? Slocum couldn't imagine what robbery of the Mexican National Mint might act as diversion for, but it had to be significant.

He turned his chestnut's head in the direction taken by El Jéfe. Slocum rode quickly but kept a sharp eye out for the him. It would be easy to miss him in the darkness. But it wasn't easy to miss the towering spire of the Monterrey Cathedral ahead. Slocum slowed and studied the church. How many lives had been lost building it, he didn't know. The huge beams had been hoisted into place on the backs of *los Indios* impressed to service by the Spanish.

Two horses were tethered outside the church. Slocum recognized the fancy silver chasing on El Jéfe's saddle, and the other horse might be Belicia's. This seemed a strange time to go pray, if that was what they were doing.

Somehow, he didn't think they were taking time to confess their sins.

Slocum rode around to the side of the cathedral, dismounted and checked his Colt Navy to be sure it carried six loads. He wasn't looking for trouble, but he hadn't thought a bandido would stop at a church on the way out of town after robbing the mint, either. Slocum had to be ready for anything. He tried to peer into a small window, but the view was restricted to an empty vestibule. He went to another window, this one of stained glass. Though he saw nothing in the room on the other side, he heard movement.

Prying open one side of the window, he got his fingers behind the glass and pulled. He tried not to make much noise but the screeching as the window frame wrenched free of the plaster was loud enough to awaken the dead. Knowing that he was better off getting in and not prolonging this noise, Slocum put one foot against the exterior wall and heaved hard. A single loud crash resulted and the window flew free to crash onto the ground, shattering into a hundred pieces.

He looked into the room and saw two dark figures on the floor. He slid through the opening and dropped into a crouch, pistol leveled. The dark forms kicked and jerked about. Muffled noises came from their general direction, prompting Slocum to even more caution. He duck-walked to one and reached out, touching coarse cloth.

"I'll be damned," he muttered, hardly aware of the blasphemy of swearing in a church. A priest had been hogtied and gagged. A quick check showed the second lump was another priest. Imploring eyes looked up at him. Slocum shook his head and put his finger to his mouth, urging them to be quiet. He wasn't going to free the priests until he found out what El Jéfe and Belicia were up to.

He found the narrow door leading into the cathedral. The door came out to one side of the main altar. Belicia and El Jéfe stood in the middle of the church, arguing hotly. She waved her hands and raised her voice. El Jéfe said something that made her quiet down a mite, but Slocum wasn't able to catch the drift of the argument from this distance.

Crouching once again, he made his way out to the first row of pews near a bank of lighted candles. The smoke from the flames almost made him choke. He pushed his free hand over his mouth to keep from revealing himself with a cough. Belicia hadn't come to the cathedral for any honest purpose. And most people's avarice would have been satisfied by the incredible load of silver already on its way north into the central mountains.

Slocum worked his way closer until he could hear Belicia's whispered arguments.

"It's here. It *must* be. I will not leave without it."

"We have no more time. You have sought it long enough. *Los soldados*," he pleaded, reaching out to take both her hands in his. She pulled away angrily. El Jéfe continued as if he hadn't noticed her determination. "They will come soon. They will come from Durango, they will come from the mountains and Mexico City, but they will come. And they will want our heads."

"You go. I refuse to leave until it is once more in my hands."

El Jéfe threw up his hands in defeat. "I cannot leave you. I will help you look, but where might it be? You have looked everywhere these past twenty minutes."

Slocum settled down, not sure what they sought. Belicia stormed past him and never noticed. El Jéfe followed but he didn't see Slocum, either. The pair went to the chancel and began at one end, working across, studying every religious item and discarding it.

"A hidden compartment. That's where those *pendejos* might have hidden it." Belicia was furious. She put her hands on her hips and slowly turned to study every nook and cranny of the large cathedral's nave. She didn't find what she was searching for and turned back. Slocum chanced a quick peek around the pew and saw her and El Jéfe on their knees in front of the altar. He thought they were praying, then saw they had pried loose one corner of the wood front.

El Jéfe grunted as he heaved and ripped loose the facade. He tossed the wooden sheet aside to point to a hollow spot.

"There is nothing, Belicia. Come, I beg you, let's leave. We have so little time."

"No!" Belicia shot to her feet and cried, "I'll torture those worthless, thieving priests. They will not keep it. They know were it is, and they will tell me!"

She whipped out a thin, vicious looking knife. Slocum almost called out to her then, telling her they'd be in a world of trouble if she carved up priests. Robbing the mint sent waves all the way to Mexico City and Porfirio Diaz himself, but torturing and killing priests got the entire countryside riled.

El Jéfe stopped her, his hand wrapping around her wrist and forcing it back until she dropped the blade. He bent and picked up the knife, studied her angry face, then slipped it into his leather belt.

"I'll keep this, for the moment," he said.

"I will not leave until I find it," she said, more than a hint of viciousness in her tone. Belicia was determined, and Slocum admired El Jéfe's courage all the more facing her like this.

He shrugged and turned back to ripping apart the altar, hunting for whatever it was they sought. Belicia went to the rear of the chancel, stared up at a huge crucifix, then turned and followed the baleful gaze to a spot just behind the altar railing. She went to it, then cried out in joy.

"José, José, this is it! I know it is!" She made room for him to use the knife on a section of railing. Instead of painful wood screeching as there had been when El Jéfe destroyed the front of the altar,

Slocum heard only a tiny click as the hidden chamber opened.

"There it is! I knew they had it, I knew they did!"

Slocum couldn't see what they coveted so, but he knew it must be special. He worked his way down the line of pews and headed for the vestibule to get a better view. Belicia held a two-foot-tall jewel and gold-encrusted wooden statue of the Virgin Mary. She pulled the santo to her breast and held it like a small child, rocking it back and forth and cooing.

"Now, Belicia, now we must go. Put it in its box." El Jéfe nervously licked his lips and looked toward the narthex, as if he had heard something Slocum hadn't.

Belicia put the statue in its reliquary and picked up the wood box, still cradling it like a young child. The expression on her face was one of ecstasy. She had found what she would trade for all the silver in the mint.

Before either El Jéfe or Belicia could leave, the huge front doors of the cathedral burst open. The rumbling echoes almost deafened Slocum as a dozen armed men poured into the church. El Jéfe and Belicia were caught in the act of stealing a religious relic.

9

This wasn't Slocum's fight. He could slip back quietly through the vestibule where the two priests were bound and gagged and duck out the window without anyone seeing him. He had everything to lose and nothing to gain by helping Belicia and José. If he cut and ran, he would be wealthy beyond his wildest dreams. Hundreds of pounds of silver was waiting for him. All he had to do was get out of the church with his skin in one piece.

He stood and started firing slow, methodical shots that scattered the men who had burst into the cathedral.

"Run for it," he called to Belicia and El Jéfe. "Through the side door, where you left the priests." He kept up the slow, accurate fire until his six-shooter's hammer fell on an empty chamber. He shoved his pistol back into its soft leather holster, then ran like hell. If he hadn't slowed the mob's advance when he did, they would have washed over the other two like the surf pounding along the beach.

He stumbled when a priest reached out and grabbed his ankle. Slocum tried kicking free, but the priest's grip was too strong. He had worked himself free of his ropes in time to catch one of his church's defilers. Slocum couldn't fire; his six-gun was empty. And the priest hung on with a ferocity that belied his calling.

A knife flashed brightly as it cartwheeled past his ear. It landed with a dull thud in the priest's arm. The pressure on Slocum's ankle relaxed as the hand lost its strength.

"He is not dead, if that matters to you," El Jéfe said through the window. "Will you come now? The men with the shotguns do not look friendly."

Slocum slithered through the window as a bullet winged over his head. Then the roar from firing rifles and shotguns almost deafened him. He had torn the window free of its frame. Now bullets and 00 buckshot tore the wall apart. He ran for all he was worth, reaching his horse just as some of the mob came back through the front doors. More bullets sought his flesh in the darkness, but distance aided him now. He was too far from the men firing at him for any but a lucky shot to hit him. Bending low, he put his heels to the chestnut's flanks, urging the horse to all the speed she was capable of giving.

The people of Monterrey wouldn't take kindly to him if they caught him. Robbing the mint, stealing from the cathedral, injuring a priest, those were crimes that would get him torn apart by an angry mob. He bent lower and kept up his headlong pace through the city's streets. Dying on the spot might be better, though, than rotting in any Mexican prison. They were even worse than Yuma Territorial Penitentiary.

Slocum overtook Belicia and El Jéfe a few miles outside town. Their horses had faltered and threatened to die under them if they kept up their wild gallop. Slocum had paced his horse better and there was still a mile or two left in the straining animal, but he slowed and finally came to a halt beside the bandido leader.

"You saved our skins, Señor Slocum," El Jéfe said. "Thank you for this."

"What was it you stole from the church? It made a raft of people mad at you."

Belicia let out a screech that startled an owl in a nearby juniper tree. The bird let out a call of its own and fluttered into the darkness. She bobbed up and down in the saddle and continued to let out incoherent noises.

"She gets so upset because of this," El Jéfe said.

"It was stolen from my people. They did it, those, those, priests!" Belicia began sputtering again. Slocum wasn't sure what the real story was, but the woman obviously felt aggrieved and the injured party. "I want to return it to its proper place where common people can worship, not some fabulous cathedral open only to *los ricos*."

Again Slocum wondered at her background. She was not of the common people she felt so strongly about. Neither was El Jéfe, but this wasn't the time to find out backgrounds. Slocum didn't have to be in touch with the saints to know the soldiers would be hot on their trail. The mint robbery would draw the *Federales* from all over, and the theft from a cathedral would incite the countryside. Mexico was getting less healthy for them by the minute.

"Where were you supposed to go with Hughes?" Slocum asked.

"There is no safe place in my country," El Jéfe said. "We were to cross the border and go into the section of New Mexico you call 'the boot heel.' Do you know the area?"

Slocum did. New Mexico Territory was almost a perfect square when it was laid out on a map, all except a segment in the southwest corner. There the surveyors had jogged twice, giving the region the look of a boot heel. It was a rough section, filled with mountains, wandering valleys and more than a few gold and silver mines. Some copper was mined to the north and the entire area was crawling with Jicarilla Apaches. It was hard country and exactly the place needed for the Hughes Bunch to rendezvous with the Estrada Gang.

"It is not in our country," El Jéfe went on, "and provides us with some cover."

"There's more than a little danger for us, though," Slocum said. "We stole the burros from an army station. They won't forget any time soon." He cocked his head to one side and heard horses' hooves thundering in the distance. The hounds were already after the fox. Slocum cursed. He had hoped it would take until morning, or later, for effective pursuit to develop. By then he could have been a dozen miles farther down the road toward Hughes and the pack train of silver coins.

"I, too, hear them," said El Jéfe. "We must rejoin Hughes and the others for protection."

"We ought to set a decoy," Slocum said.

"The Virgin Mary!" cried Belicia. "They will take it back if they find us. I will not allow it. I will die before ever returning it to those pigs!"

"We have many troubles," El Jéfe said with a sigh of resignation. "If they find us this quickly, there might be hundreds seeking us. That is not good."

"We can fight them off," Slocum said, thinking hard. "We might have to lay a false trail to split their pursuit, but we can do it. As far as most people in the countryside know, Hughes is just a guano merchant and not worthy of a second glance. If he did it right getting to Monterrey, no one will pay any attention to him on his way out of the country."

"That is so, but there are twice as many in the party returning north. That would draw comment."

Belicia clutched the reliquary holding the gold and bejeweled wood santo of the Virgin Mary. She wouldn't be much good if they tried to leave it to distract the posse on their trail. Just suggesting such a diversion would turn her into a hellcat, and arguing that thirty burros laden with silver was a better reward would never set well with her. This was a religious icon and carried more consideration for her than mere wealth.

"We've got to join up with the pack train to let Hughes know what he's up against," Slocum said. "But there's no reason we should go directly. Do you know the route he's taking to the border?" Slocum saw El Jéfe shake his head no. He had sent most of his men with the Hughes Bunch to keep them honest and that was all he knew, except the meeting place in New Mexico's boot heel.

"Get your horses walking that way," Slocum said, hearing the faint gurgle of a stream. "We might delay them if they are tracking us, and if they're following the road thinking we'll stick to it, we can lose them in a few minutes."

El Jéfe and Belicia started off, the woman still clinging to the plain wooden box with the statue. She would have to be killed to pry it loose, and Slocum knew the mob behind them was likely to do just that. Roughing up a priest, even a thieving one, was never a good idea. People didn't understand.

The flow was too shallow for Slocum's liking. He pointed downstream. El Jéfe silently followed. Belicia cooed to the statue as if it were a thing alive. They splashed along for almost ten minutes before Slocum stopped them to listen for sounds of pursuit. The gurgling stream covered many small noises but he thought he heard men calling to each other about where they had entered the stream. Slocum signaled that he wanted to go uphill, inland and away from the road. El Jéfe followed without question but Belicia wanted to argue.

"This must be returned to its rightful place," she insisted. "There is no time, no time to waste. We must go now."

"You're not thinking straight," Slocum warned. "They'll kill you within an hour, and the relic will never get back to its rightful owner."

"It belongs to my village. I have the duty, the obligation to return the Virgin to my people."

The way she spoke told Slocum he had been right. She was talking about the *peones* in some village as if they were her personal servants. Belicia might be on some mission, but

she did it out of duty to those she considered incapable of
retrieving their own stolen santo. Slocum struggled for the
term he had heard used once: noblesse oblige, the duty of
a master to a peasant.

"First, we get away," he said. The struggle up the hill
on their tired horses was almost too much. They stumbled
repeatedly in the darkness, but they reached the summit.
Slocum wasn't sure if he was glad to see a road running
down the valley on the far side. If they could lose themselves
in the wilderness, that was for the best. He knew he was better
at hiding a trail than anyone in the posse behind him was at
finding the true track they'd taken.

"We are near a road leading north," El Jéfe said. "If we
take that we might find Hughes and my own men."

"They might have sentries posted along that road, too,"
Slocum said.

"You flee when no one follows," El Jéfe said. Slocum
stared at him, trying to remember when the same thought
had crossed his mind. He couldn't.

"There's good reason to run like hell," he said, but he
gave in. The three of them made their way down the steep
hill and onto the road. Slocum wanted to talk to Belicia but
this didn't seem to be the time. She was happier than he
had seen her since he'd saved her pretty neck in the church.
She had lost some of the fervor that had driven her and was
able to look ahead to returning the icon.

But he rode in silence, not wanting to start a conversation
El Jéfe might overhear. He still hadn't figured out Belicia
and the bandidos relationship. He acted as her protector at
times and lover at others.

"Ahead, they are ahead! *Mira.*" El Jéfe stood in his stirrups
and pointed toward a line of men and pack animals working
their way up the narrow road into the mountains.

Slocum wasn't sure it was Hughes and the others, but
how many long trains of burros would be on the road at
this time of night? He fumbled out his brother Robert's
watch and opened the case, peering at the face. It was

almost four in the morning. Sunrise would bathe them in revealing light in another couple of hours. It would be best to go to ground and rest then, letting any pursuit pass them by. Hiding with thirty heavily-laden burros would be a sight harder, since the animals had to be unloaded, fed, watered and kept quiet.

Keeping a burro quiet when it wanted to complain was impossible. Slocum knew they would have to rely on their rifles if any posse found them. Still, it would be good to see what he had gone to so much trouble to get. Silver. More silver than he had imagined existing in the entire world!

"John, I must talk with you," Belicia said, riding so close that her leg brushed his. El Jéfe was pushing his horse to reach the pack train. He was anxious to be sure all was well with the get from his robbery. Slocum didn't fault him for that.

"This isn't the time," he said. Something worried him but he couldn't put his finger on it. Being distracted by the lovely woman only added to his sense of uneasiness.

"I had to do this, John. To me the silver means nothing. But this is my heart, my soul, everything. I pledged on my mother's grave that I would return it." Again Slocum saw the glow in the woman's eyes.

"You did it," he said, looking around. The burros were snorting and snuffling just ahead and El Jéfe called to Paco. Doc Neal rode back to see what the commotion was, and the word was passed along to Hughes that they had company.

"Please, we can—"

Slocum cut her off with a brusque wave of his hand. "Later. Something's wrong." He put his heels to his tired horse's flanks and hurried forward to talk with Hughes. The leader of the Hughes Bunch looked like the cat that had just eaten the canary. Slocum almost imagined feathers on the man's lips.

"You made it, Slocum. We were wondering about you. Not about him, though." Hughes tipped his head in El Jéfe's direction. "You didn't go out of your way to save him, did you?"

"It's a long story. Do you have anybody out scouting?"

"No need. We're simple guano dealers. A couple *Federales* passed us by on the road and never gave a second look. This is a great disguise. Who wants to paw through sacks they think are loaded with shit?" Hughes laughed, then got the glum expression on his face when he saw Slocum wasn't joining in. Slocum wasn't sure he didn't prefer the man's usual dour look to him being so damned happy. When he was grinning he wasn't thinking straight.

"The posse was hot on our heels, and they suddenly vanished, just like they knew where we were going."

"What are you saying, Slocum?"

"They might have put the three of us with you and taken a shortcut. I don't know these hills too well, and El Jéfe was just going along for the ride. He had other things on his mind." Slocum looked over his shoulder to where Belicia had dismounted and was covering the reliquary with a blanket to protect it against dew.

"You think we're riding into the jaws of a trap?"

"Won't hurt to send somebody a few miles down the road to check," Slocum said.

"Don't like sending one of the bunch," Hughes allowed. "I don't trust those Mexican varmints."

Slocum had been wrong about a double-cross inside the mint. He didn't see it in the cards now. El Jéfe seemed honest enough when he talked of getting to the boot heel and divvying up the take. Even ordinary avarice was sated at the sight of so much silver.

"We got to get across the border quick," Slocum said. He always relied on his instinct, and something made the hair on the back of his neck crawl now. Danger was near.

"We can take a different road," Hughes said. "There's a fork not a mile back. We turn the burros around and take it. Adds a few miles to the trip and puts us on rougher road, but—"

"Do it," Slocum said. "Send somebody out to scout, just to be sure."

The plan to backtrack a mile and keep moving was met with groans of displeasure, but Sandy King, Zwing Hunt and Doc Neal obeyed. Curly Bill was more vocal about not liking it.

"He's throwed in with them," the killer said. "He wants to drive us into the ground so him and his new buddies can take us easy."

Slocum was too tired to argue. "Just scout ahead a mile or two. If there's nothing there, come back and tell us and we'll stay on this road."

"Do it, Bill," ordered Hughes. "It won't take that long, and we can't vanish on you with your share. There's too damned much of it to do that."

Curly Bill sneered but turned his horse and galloped off. Slocum heaved a sigh, then set to checking his six-shooter and Winchester. He was seldom wrong when it came to such gut feelings. Slocum wondered if he ought to warn El Jéfe and Belicia to stay saddled and ready to fight. They were arguing again, about what he couldn't tell. Disturbing them seemed pointless.

"They're comin'!" came the shout from down the road. "Damn me if there ain't a hundred of 'em!" Curly Bill rode like all the demons of hell were nipping at his heels. "*Federales*. Never seen so many of them."

"We can hold them off and let the burros get on the other road, then decoy them," Slocum said, thinking fast.

"We will do it," El Jéfe said. "They will see us, know we are *Los Bandidos de la Estrada* and consider us fair game. That will give you the chance to cross the border."

Slocum looked at the man with new admiration. Everything El Jéfe said was right. The *Federales* had no reason to go after Americans since they had to be coming from Durango. He doubted if word of the Monterrey robbery had reached the garrison there yet, but it might have. Mexican telegraphy wasn't anywhere near as reliable as north of the

border, but the accursed machine might have worked this
time and spread news of the mint's robbery.

"Take her with you," El Jéfe said. His voice was level,
but there was a set to his jaw that betrayed his emotion.
"She will be safer across the border."

Slocum nodded agreement. Curly Bill continued to shout
and raise a ruckus, sure to get the *Federales* on their trail.
Hughes went to quiet the man and get him riding back to
the pack train. El Jéfe was already putting his silver rowls
to his horse's sides.

"The soldiers! They come, they come!" went up the cry
from El Jéfe's bandidos. Belicia jerked around, startled. She
quickly climbed back into the saddle and turned her pony's
face toward the oncoming wave of *Federales*.

"Ride, Belicia," Slocum urged. "Join the others with the
pack train and José will meet us in New Mexico." She got
her horse into a trot, then suddenly stood in the stirrups and
reined back. Slocum saw the problem instantly. She had left
the statue of the Virgin Mary in its reliquary under the tree.
The tattered blanket she had it shrouded in flapped slightly
in the night breeze.

"I will get it," El Jéfe cried. "Ride north, Belicia, ride
north!" The bandido leader bent over and gathered the
statue, placing it across the saddle in front of him. Slocum
cut Belicia off and kept her from trying to fetch the statue.
Already the lead element of the *Federales'* column was in
sight and their carbines were being unlimbered. A ragged
volley that did nothing more than spook the horses ripped
through the trees and blew a few leaves apart.

"He'll take good care of it, Belicia. We've got to
go," Slocum cried. "There's no way to fight them
all."

"The Virgin," moaned Belicia. She saw that El Jéfe had
already engaged the leading soldier, taking him out of the
saddle with a well-placed shot. The bandido leader reared
his horse, shouted something obscene in Spanish and raced
away through the woods.

The rest of the Estrada Gang galloped up the hill and joined the battle, covering their leader's escape with the statue. Then they broke rank and followed.

"There isn't anything you can do without getting killed, Belicia," Slocum told her. He held her horse's reins and tried to quiet his own as they hid in a brushy area. The *Federales* never saw them as they tore off in hot pursuit of *Los Bandidos de la Estrada*. Belicia hung her head and cried at having lost the statue.

Or was it El Jéfe she mourned for? Slocum didn't know. When the last of the *Federales* vanished, he walked his horse through the brush and started down the road to the fork to follow the Hughes Bunch and the silver-laden burros north to the border. Belicia rode beside him, crying softly.

10

"Will he be all right?" Belicia asked. "The *Federales* are tenacious once they get a scent."

Slocum had no answer. They had been dodging all night and dawn was turning the horizon pink. He was about ready to fall asleep in the saddle, but he wanted to keep on. They had somehow missed the turnoff in the road and hadn't overtaken Hughes and the pack train of silver-laden burros. This didn't bother him unduly. If anything, he counted it as a stroke of luck. He had evaded the *Federales*; none trailed him, but if their luck turned bad and they met another patrol, getting lost again in the forest would be easier without the burros to contend with.

"José is clever," she went on, as if he had answered. "He will avoid them. He knows these hills well. We grew up here."

"Tell me about him," Slocum said, hoping to keep her occupied as they rode. He tried to figure how much longer they could continue before the horses rebelled. Not much, he decided. Already his chestnut was stumbling on level patches of stone and faltering when the roadway steepened.

"He will be all right?" she asked again. "He has the Virgin Mary. It has to be returned."

"That's your only involvement in the robbery, isn't it? You used the theft from the mint as diversion. Did El Jéfe promise you any of the silver?"

"I want nothing from it. The statue is everything. My oath is sacred. The statue came from Spain two hundred years ago and is thrice blessed by the Pope. And miracles occur near it."

Slocum didn't much believe in miracles but knew people who did. He wasn't going to argue a matter of faith. He preferred to believe a fast gun and an accurate first shot were better than any miracle; but if Belicia thought the statue carried powers beyond the gold and jewels encrusting it, that was fine with him.

"Where does it go? How'd it come to be stolen?"

"It was hidden during the Inquisition and came to protect a small village high in the mountains. My ancestors moved to this town and prospered. Don Alberto, my father, was showered with great good fortune. Then *they* stole it."

"The priests at the Monterrey Cathedral?" Slocum asked. "Why would they steal it?" He was thinking of gold and jewels and the fancy trappings inside the church. Even for a priest who had taken a vow of poverty, the statue would have little value compared with most of the relics inside the church.

"They claim it is theirs by right. They lie. They want it because the Virgin Mary acts through it to perform miraculous cures. They want to increase their power in Monterrey by curing those who work for Diaz of their maladies. They want to pervert its goodness for their own vile purposes."

Slocum saw that the issue mixed politics as well as religion, and probably more than a hint of simple greed, too. He couldn't believe any man could look at the statue and not covet its jewels and gold. But there was something more that Belicia hadn't told him. He waited and she finally managed to choke out the words.

"The day after it was stolen from the simple church in Las Lagrimas de Oro, my mother fell ill. She died on the day that news arrived that the statue was in the Cathedral of Monterrey. They killed my mother and broke my father's heart. They doomed the entire countryside around Las Lagrimas. Drought has plagued us since the gentle Virgin Mary has been gone."

"Las Lagrimas de Oro? Your village?" Slocum had never heard of it but that wasn't too surprising. Most of the out-of-the-way towns were unknown to him. "Tears of Gold?"

"The name was changed after the Virgin came to reside in our church. She weeps golden tears. Touching the tear will cure any illness, no matter how severe. Prayers are answered when she cries, and there was never a drought or flood in more than two hundred years. Now nothing but woe has befallen my family and my people."

Slocum wanted to turn the conversation around to Belicia's relationship with El Jéfe, but the sound of gunfire ahead caused him to rein back. They had to take cover immediately. He dismounted and led his exhausted horse to the shelter of a thicket. Belicia followed, her horse stumbling as it went. A small stream provided water for the animals while Slocum stood guard.

A small patrol of *Federales* rode past, never bothering to look at the ground for spoor. Slocum kept watch another few minutes but the danger had passed. He turned to ask Belicia if she wanted to camp during the day and continue riding at sundown when he saw she had already answered. She was curled up in the roots of a tree, her head resting on her arm. She slept peacefully, the frantic ride to escape already erased from her face.

Slocum unsaddled the horses, rubbed them down and pulled them back from the water to keep them from bloating. Only after he had securely fastened their reins to a limb allowing them to graze on some lush grass did he unroll his own blanket and lie down. Sleep was elusive. He kept thinking of Belicia and El Jéfe, the Virgin Mary and more silver than he had ever dreamed about stealing. He finally slept, but he was plagued by legions of *Federales* and the U.S. Cavalry charging him as he crossed the border.

After Belicia's horse pulled up lame just after starting out that evening, they had to wait two days before the animal could support her weight. Slocum hated the delay but saw no way to avoid it. Stealing another horse wasn't a good idea, even if there had been any nearby. And riding double on his chestnut was out of the question. He had pushed the horse to its limit, and it could carry him and no more. By the time Slocum found the trail left by the north-bound pack train, he thought the Hughes Bunch might already be in the boot heel.

Slocum glanced at the storm cloud studded sky and shivered. He began worrying because he hadn't seen any trace of the Estrada Gang. He either had to track Hughes and the burros or find El Jéfe to learn of the rendezvous point. If it rained, he would lose the trail. And where could he possibly find the wily Mexican bandido?

"You can find the spot where we are to meet?" Belicia asked.

"Reckon so, if it doesn't rain too hard too fast. If it turns into a frog strangler, there's no way I'll be able to find Hughes."

"He did not trust you with the location? You, his right hand man?"

Belicia seemed to find this amusing. Slocum vowed he would track Hughes down to the far side of the moon if he had to. Five hundred pounds of silver—more!—was too much to allow to slip through his fingers.

"I'm not his right hand man. Curly Bill comes closest to that. I didn't join up until a couple months back." Slocum considered how much water had run under the bridge in that time. Several minor robberies like the cavalry payroll, then the two-week stint in Mexico preparing for the Monterrey robbery.

"El Jéfe tells me everything," Belicia said, bragging.

"I don't suppose he happened to mention where he was going to find Hughes?"

"But of course he did. That way, along the Old Fronteras Road," she said pointing. "We are almost in Arizona, no?"

Slocum didn't rightly know if they were in Arizona or New Mexico and it didn't much matter. They had gone northwesterly through Chihuahua to avoid the *Federales* rather than heading north for Texas and might have gone far enough west to be in Arizona now. All the Sonora Desert was hotter than Hades and so dry he had to prime himself to spit.

"You knew all along where he was headed?" Slocum wondered at the other things the woman might know. They had ridden mostly in silence the past few days because both had needed the time alone, though they were heading in the same direction.

"Generally, yes," she said. "José is a man of habit. There are so few places he would agree to meet north of the border."

"What is it between the two of you?" Slocum asked. He couldn't look her square in the eye as he spoke. He scanned the horizon, hoping to find a spot that looked cooler than the inferno where they were. He didn't find anywhere that looked encouraging, but going along the Old Fronteras Road would soon take them into the Peloncillo Mountains where it had to be cooler, both in temperature and pursuit by the law.

"There!" she cried suddenly. "Do you see it? A cloud of dust rising along the road."

Slocum turned in the direction Belicia pointed and saw the commotion. For a dust cloud that big, it had to be either a stagecoach racing along at breakneck speed or a long line of pack animals. He doubted any driver would kill his team racing them in this heat. That left only the Hughes Bunch and the burros laden with silver.

"They are not so far. Let us ride quickly. I must see if José has rejoined them."

Once again, Belicia was obsessed with her statue of the Virgin Mary and Slocum saw he wasn't going to get any information from her. That might be for the best. She was from a different social class. She belonged on the rancho, with servants and *peones* to do her bidding. That she had taken it upon herself to perform this religious quest didn't change her station in life. Her father, Don Alberto, was the next to last of a chain running back to the Spanish Conquest. Slocum didn't fit into her life.

So why did a bandit chief? Slocum might never find out. He turned his chestnut's head and trotted to one side of the alkali track Belicia had called the Old Fronteras Road. She was eager to join El Jéfe and retrieve her precious statue. He was as eager to get his cut from the mint robbery and take off. Staying with the Hughes Bunch held no attraction for him now. The only reason to steal was to get rich, and they had all done that beyond their wildest expectations.

Twenty minutes later they overtook the slower moving burros. Belicia tried not to show her disappointment when it was apparent only Paco and two others from the Estrada Gang rode with the caravan.

"Where's El Jéfe?" Slocum asked Hughes after they had gotten their greetings out of the way. "I figured he would be the first one across the border."

"Waiting for us up in the hills," Hughes said. "We'll be there just after sundown. Glad you made it, Slocum."

The grimness in Hughes' words put Slocum on edge. Something was wrong, and he didn't know what it could be.

"The law give you any trouble, here or south of the border?"

"We been seein' signs of a cavalry troop, but nothing we can't handle. And the *Federales* never came within a country mile of us after we split from you outside Monterrey,"

Hughes said. "We had a pure ten days of easy travellin'. I'm worried, though."

"About what?" Slocum wanted Jim Hughes to open up and tell him. He was getting edgy himself, looking around and jumping at shadows.

"Later. When we get to the rendezvous." Hughes urged his horse ahead, leaving Slocum to ride alone and stew in his own thoughts. He couldn't figure out what had made Hughes so edgy, but it put him into a mood, too. Slocum checked the Colt Navy at his hip, making sure he had all six cylinders loaded, just in case.

Nightfall brought blessed coolness with it. They had climbed steadily into the Peloncillos and the dampness of mountain air. Somewhat revived, Slocum still didn't relax. Hughes wasn't as happy as a man ought to be riding along with three or four tons of silver, but this was more like his usual demeanor. Only when he had first spoken of the chance of robbing the Monterrey Mint had he seemed to enjoy himself. Still, Slocum was uncomfortable with the atmosphere. He got even more worried when they rode into the camp the Estrada Gang had set up. Two small cooking fires blazed and pots of beans bubbled, making his mouth water. Small loaves of bread had been baked in the ashes and the entire campsite should have put his worry to rest.

If anything, it made him even more wary.

"The silver!" cried El Jéfe. "It has come. Thank you, Paco. *Grácias*, for you have brought it all to me!"

Belicia rode directly to El Jéfe and started to dismount. Slocum could see the questions about the statue on her lips. But she never got a chance to say a word. Half a dozen shots rang out, then six more, and then the air filled with white smoke. Cries of dying men mingled with the neighing of frightened horses, and Slocum didn't know what the hell was happening.

11

Slocum jumped off his frightened horse and dived for cover, not sure who was doing the firing or who to take a potshot at. He slithered like a snake until he got to the safety of a juniper and pulled himself up behind it. One of El Jéfe's men ran past him, bleeding from three wounds. The way he limped, he might have taken a fourth slug in the thigh. Before Slocum could call to him and get him under cover, a singing rifle bullet took the top off the man's head. Blood and brains spewed forth in a gruesome geyser.

Slocum hunkered down, his Colt ready for action. Who was firing on them? The cavalry? He didn't think the *Federales* had ambushed them. They had been noisy and loved blowing bugle charges and crunching along so even a blind and deaf man could spot them. That left only Apaches. The Jicarillas and Mescaleros didn't like the white man intruding on their traditional land, but both groups had been put on the reservations at Bosque Redondo. A renegade band might have found the camp, but Slocum didn't think so. The Apaches preferred to attack when they could see what they were doing. A man's soul was trapped to wander for all eternity if he died in battle after darkness fell.

Slocum thanked his lucky stars the Comanches had been subdued years earlier. They didn't care when they lifted a white man's scalp; morning, noon or night was just fine. But who was doing all the firing?

Chancing a quick glance from behind the tree's thick bole, Slocum saw dim figures walking through the clearing smoke. The gunfire had died down. An occasional pistol report sounded, but the barrage was past. Who had emerged the victor? Slocum waited. He'd fight like a Comanche to keep his share of the silver.

"That got 'em, men," came Jim Hughes' somber voice. "They never knew what hit 'em. You boys done good, real good." The leader of the Hughes Bunch kicked one fallen Estrada, rolling him onto his back so his arms flopped out on either side, as if he had been crucified. Sightless eyes stared up into the twilight. Hughes put a round into the man's gut, just for spite.

Slocum moved from behind the tree, his six-shooter ready. He hadn't fired; that gave him an edge over the others. He doubted a single one of the Hughes Bunch had a full cylinder or magazine in his weapon. But it was still five of them against only one of him. All it took to kill any man was one well-placed slug.

"There you are. Wondered what happened to you, Slocum. You get spooked or something?" asked Hughes.

"The damned coward tried to cut and run, that's what happened," Curly Bill called out. Smoke and blood had turned Curly Bill into a savage. His eyes were wide and the whites shone like rings in his blackened, bloodied face. He waved his rifle around wildly and had a brace of pistols thrust into his belt. Slocum estimated his odds. He could take Curly Bill, then shoot Jim Hughes before either leveled his gun.

"She got away!" came Doc Neal's cry. "Her and their damned leader. They got away!"

"There's another what sneaked off," spoke up Zwing Hunt. "I hit him and thought he was a goner, but he snuck off."

"Can't even bushwhack a man right," grumbled Hughes. "You ought to be more like Bill here. He got his men."

To make his point, Curly Bill fired another round into the Estrada whose head was well nigh blown off. He laughed like a crazy man and went roaming the scene of the slaughter for anyone who might still be alive.

"What went wrong?" asked Slocum. "Did they try to steal the silver?"

"Try? Hell, no, they didn't try, but they were planning on it. You warned me."

"I must have been wrong. I thought they'd try to take it when we were inside the mint. El Jéfe looked downright pleased we'd been so successful there. He even saved my life."

"His problem," Hughes grumbled. "I figured they were going to try to take the silver, so what the hell? Beat 'em to it. I had to wait to get here to be sure all their gang was in one place. That big one—Paco—he was my real worry. He fought like ten men on the way. We ran into a cavalry unit when we crossed the border. Didn't want to tangle with him."

"So you shot him in the back?" Slocum asked, cold fury building. El Jéfe had played straight with them. There was no call for Hughes to double-cross the Mexicans.

"Naw, I let Curly Bill do it. He gets a kick out of seeing a man kick around in the dust before he dies. So what are you whining about, Slocum? This means twice the silver for us. Doesn't half a ton of silver make shooting a few bullets worthwhile?"

"We couldn't have done it without them," Slocum said, realizing that he could have been cut down in the barrage and nobody in the Hughes Bunch would have done more than spit on his corpse.

"What are you, some kind of Mexican-lover?" Hughes

turned and was starting to consider his chances at shooting down Slocum when Sandy King came riding up and broke the tension.

"Jim, it *was* El Jéfe who got away. Him and the woman and one other. We got to find them quick."

"Why bother?" asked Slocum. "What can they do now?"

"The cavalry," said King. "He can go fetch the cavalry and get them down on our necks. He'll lose the silver but he'll get his revenge. We'll all swing."

"Sandy's right," said Hughes. "The Mexican isn't wanted north of the border. The cavalry might not like dealing with him but to bring in the Hughes Bunch, they'd deal with the devil himself. We got to stop him quick."

"Unless you got some objections, Slocum." Curly Bill had returned. He had discarded his rifle and had both six-shooters in his hands. Any advantage Slocum might have had was gone now. Curly Bill was quick and accurate. Hughes was willing to put a slug through his head just because he was arguing over murdering *Los Bandidos de la Estrada*. And Sandy King would go along with Hughes.

"A half ton of silver goes a long ways toward soothing my ruffled feathers," Slocum said, still gauging his chances. If anything changed, he'd have to act. He was the newcomer to the gang, and they were forming ranks against him because he had spoken against the backshooting double-cross.

"Then why don't you just hightail it after El Jéfe and the other two and bring 'em back?" asked Hughes. "You're about the best tracker we got. El Jéfe might decide to hide his trail."

"Why don't we just divvy up the take and go our separate ways? There're six of us. I'll just take five burros and—"

"No!" Hughes glowered at him. "We don't split up, not yet. We'd get picked off one by one by the cavalry. It's best if we keep the burros in one pack train because we can guard it easier. You want some gang of yahoos sticking you up an hour after you take off on your own?"

"What's the plan?" Slocum asked, still looking for an angle that would save both his own hide and his share of the silver. The longer he kept Hughes talking, the better chance he had of staying alive. And alive, he could work out how to get the silver.

"You track down El Jéfe, the woman and the other Estrada. Bring them back and—"

"If you kill them, you got to bring us proof other than your word. Their scalps will do," cut in Curly Bill. "Unless you're too squeamish for that, Slocum."

"I'll find them and bring them back," Slocum said. "Here?"

"We got to keep moving," Hughes said. "The cavalry might be on our trail. The sound of gunfire might draw them to this spot. We'll keep moving toward Silver City." Hughes almost smiled at the irony of the town's name. "Don't be too long, Slocum, because we can't stay too long anywhere."

"The silver will be with you?"

"Slocum, what are we going to do? Spirit it away? There's too much for that. We aren't going to steal your cut. We're just protecting it while you go do what you're best at. Unless you don't trust us any more." Hughes widened his stance and got ready for gunplay.

Slocum saw Hughes wanted a showdown now. He might stay alive a few minutes longer by playing along with them. They might even think he'd ride away and completely turn his back on the silver, thankful for preserving his life. For some men, that might be an acceptable trade. If any of them really believed that, though, they were in for a shock. Slocum would get his cut, one way or the other.

"Silver City?" he asked, his eyes darting around. He saw he was alone. Even Doc Neal was siding with Hughes. Slocum had been blinded by the sheer size of their haul. He had thought it was enough for any man's greed. He hadn't realized the depths of avarice in the Hughes Bunch. Curly Bill might be the exception. Gold and silver meant nothing to him if he could kill. The blood lust that drove him would put him into an early grave sooner than greed would destroy the others, but that wouldn't mean squat to Slocum if they gunned him down on the spot to take his share.

"We'll be there," Hughes said, his frown deepening. He didn't believe Slocum would give in this easily. "We'll take good care of the silver." Hughes almost smiled at this, letting Slocum know he was being dealt out of their game. None of them had the guts to go up against him alone, and Hughes hesitated to give the word, knowing Slocum would send his first bullet into the leader's belly, but the stakes were too high to just give in. Greed was too much of a factor.

"I'll get the three of them," Slocum said. He made a point of not turning his back on either Curly Bill or Hughes and always keeping his hand near his Colt. The threat of someone dying before Slocum bit the dust held the Hughes Bunch back. Sandy King and Zwing Hunt weren't going to do anything unless Hughes ordered it, and Slocum didn't think Doc Neal would try gunning him down on his own. Even Curly Bill nervously shifted his weight from foot to foot, not sure what to do.

"See you soon," Hughes said, a sneer rippling his lip.

"See you in hell," Slocum muttered under his breath. He rode out of the camp, his horse stepping gingerly over a corpse as he made his way into the forest. Every small sound made him want to jump out of his skin, but he kept his nerves under control. To show any fear now would mean his death. The Hughes Bunch might even open fire on him just for the hell of it. There was no honor among these thieves. He wanted some protection for his back so he could take the time to think this through. Going up against all the Hughes Bunch was suicidal, but there might be another way of getting his silver.

El Jéfe and the other outlaw from the Estrada Gang would want revenge. The three of them might be able to ambush the Hughes Bunch and come out ahead. It was the only way Slocum saw to avenge himself and come out of it a rich man.

If he tried picking them off one by one, he might succeed, but Curly Bill and Jim Hughes weren't the sort of men to let him do it more than once. They'd hunt him down and he'd have to be damned sure he could get them first.

Slocum checked his saddlebags for ammo and found the supply wanting. There wasn't time to ride into a nearby town and get more, even if he could find a town in the vicinity. There were several places he'd heard about, but Silver City was the closest thing to a big town where he could be sure of getting what he needed. And he doubted Hughes would ever end up in Silver City.

He started following El Jéfe's trail in earnest. The quicker he found the bandido, the sooner they could get back his share of the Monterrey silver.

For a man fleeing for his life, El Jéfe did a good job of obscuring his trail. He used several tricks that were immediately obvious to Slocum, but then he'd pull a stunt that any Apache would find puzzling. Slocum spent the better part of the day circling, looking carefully at the ground and trying to decide where the man had run.

Once, Slocum got lucky and found a piece of Belicia's blouse on a thorn bush. This kept him on the trail long enough to pick up more spoor. A horse had deposited a pile of manure that was still warm. El Jéfe couldn't be more than a half hour ahead. Slocum rode on cautiously. There wasn't any way for the bandido to know Slocum hadn't been part of the treacherous ambush. Slocum slumped in the saddle when he saw the ground ahead.

The trail split, one going south and the other continuing into the Peloncillo Mountains. Slocum had to decide which track to follow. He turned his chestnut's head south and put his heels into the animal's flanks. Overtaking the fleeing outlaw was foremost in his mind now. If he took too long, the Hughes Bunch might vanish into thin air with the silver. The mountains had dozens of branching canyons, small valleys and long river-cut meadows where ten times

as much silver might be hidden. More than once Slocum
thought of doubling back and taking care of the Hughes
Bunch by himself.

Lack of ammunition and the sheer riskiness of doing it
alone kept him on El Jéfe's trail. He thought he'd overtaken
the bandido just before twilight but found himself following
a track of unshod horses. Slocum cursed his bad luck. He'd
stumbled across a band of Apaches, probably just escaped
from the reservation. He hoped El Jéfe hadn't run afoul
of them. The Indians didn't cotton much to Americans or
Mexicans invading their territory.

Slocum shuddered at what they might do to Belicia. All
her belief in the healing power of the statue of the Virgin
Mary wouldn't come close to saving her.

He backtracked and found the chopped up grass and
confusing spoor that had caused him to miss the trail, but
by this time it was too dark to travel further. Making a cold
camp and sleeping fitfully, Slocum was up before dawn,
saddled and moving in the direction El Jéfe had taken. If
he didn't find the man before noon, Slocum had to admit
the chase would be futile. He'd have to return to find the
Hughes Bunch and do what he could to get his share.

An hour down the winding dirt path, Slocum's heart
skipped a beat when he saw how the hoofprints of El Jéfe's
horse mingled with those of a dozen or more unshod ones.
The Apaches had found themselves a victim. Slocum rode
on, every sense straining, his hand resting on the stock of
his Winchester. If he needed the rifle, he'd need it fast.

When he saw it, it took several seconds for him to
understand what he was looking at.

In the middle of the track was a head with its face turned
away from him. Slocum reined back and pulled his rifle
from its sheath. He didn't lever a round into the chamber;
the noise might draw unwanted attention from any lingering
Apaches. If he had to fight, he would. But Slocum knew he
was better off sneaking away. Fighting a band of renegades
was worse than tangling with the Hughes Bunch.

He saw no sign of Apaches as he dismounted and walked over. The man had been buried to his chin, his mouth held wide open by a large piece of wood. Ants had crawled inside the gaping mouth and had begun working on the man's innards.

Slocum wasn't sure when the man had died, but it hadn't been too long ago. And the man wasn't El Jéfe.

12

Slocum didn't recognize the man but he might have been with the Estrada Gang. The sheer fear he had felt before dying had permanently transformed the man's features and the work of the diligent ants had gone a ways toward making him unrecognizable—save to his closest relatives.

But he wasn't El Jéfe. For that Slocum heaved a sigh of relief. He needed the bandido leader if he was going to recover his fortune. And Slocum hated to admit it, even to himself, but he wanted to see Belicia one more time. The woman must be going crazy, El Jéfe having left her precious statue in the Hughes Bunch's camp. Hughes and the others might not care what was in the plain wood reliquary and simply abandon it, but if anyone opened the lid the sight of gold and jewels would cause it to be added to the load on a burro.

She wanted her statue of the Virgin Mary back, El Jéfe would want revenge, and Slocum needed his silver. The three of them might be able to work together long enough to accomplish something worthwhile. He stared at the man buried in the dirt up to his chin and shook his head. There wasn't anything he could do for this poor damned soul. If he had been alive Slocum would have used a bullet to put him out of his misery. No man survived Apache torture without being a little crazy in the head because of it.

Slocum cautiously returned to his horse and mounted, eyes darting here and there to be sure he hadn't blundered into an Apache ambush. The Indians had moved on and Slocum had to retrace the last day's travel to find where El Jéfe had parted company with this man. He wanted to turn and gallop off but held his horse down to a slow walk. He didn't feel anyone's eyes on him; his sixth sense wasn't warning him of danger from the Apaches, but there was no reason to tempt fate.

It took almost two days before he got back to the spot where he had chosen the wrong trail. El Jéfe and Belicia might be back in Mexico by now, but Slocum didn't think so. He cursed himself repeatedly for his blunder. Hughes and the silver were three days away now. The only consolation Slocum could find in his dilemma was the difficulty in moving a pack train of heavily burdened burros. Hughes had said he wouldn't be able to hide so much silver from Slocum. That was true. John Slocum would be sure of that.

The trail was cold and Slocum had to guess more and more, tracking by instinct rather than definite spoor. He found the trail curving toward the north. He wondered if he was on a wild goose chase, if El Jéfe and Belicia had managed to elude him. Then he began to understand what was going on. El Jéfe wasn't cutting directly across the route most likely taken by the Hughes Bunch. He was swinging wide and moving north to intercept where they would least expect it.

Slocum picked up the pace and spent another two days on the trail before he found fresh hoofprints in a muddy stretch beside a small creek. The deep impressions were only partially filled with water, telling him the riders had passed this way less than an hour earlier. He stopped and strained to listen. He thought he caught the soft thudding of horses making their way up a steep hill to the north of the stream.

Dismounting, Slocum let his chestnut mare rest, drink and eat some juicy grass growing along the stream. If he was less than an hour behind El Jéfe, he could overtake him. Slocum had been going over in his head the arguments to use to convince the bandido that he hadn't known about the massacre Hughes and the others had committed. No facile words would do it. Slocum knew the suspicion would run deep, maybe too deep. There had to be some action to prove to El Jéfe that Slocum was on his side.

As much as he hated to admit it, Belicia might be the key to convincing El Jéfe. He might persuade her that his help was necessary to recover her statue. El Jéfe would listen to her, and Slocum *would* help her get the relic back—especially if it meant Curly Bill, Hughes and the other back-shooting sons of bitches paid for it with their lives.

Rested and ready for the argument it would take to get in with El Jéfe again, Slocum mounted and rode at a brisk pace up the steep hill. The going got tougher by the minute but he pushed on. He wanted to overtake El Jéfe and Belicia before sundown.

The ride proved more arduous than he'd thought. Echoes from high canyon walls had deceived him into thinking they were only minutes ahead of him. They might have been a full hour away, and he had taken another hour to rest. It was growing dark in the steep-walled canyon when suddenly he came upon a small camp.

He dismounted and went to the tiny fire. Someone had eaten recently, having clubbed a small rabbit for dinner. The remains had been tossed into the fire, thinking it would put out the flames. A greasy curl of smoke rose, showing the embers were still warm. Slocum saw where a bedroll had been stretched out, but no one had lain in it. A fancy saddle proved to him that he had found El Jéfe.

Two horses were tethered nearby, one still saddled. Slocum gentled the horse to keep it from neighing. The one without the saddle had been ridden hard. Slocum examined it and saw how one leg was lame. El Jéfe had come to the end of the road on this animal.

Soft voices drifted down from deeper in the canyon. Slocum's hand flashed to his Colt Navy, drawing it in a smooth pull. He went into a crouch to minimize target area, then edged away from the horses, seeking more substantial cover. The voices rose and fell, as if the people were arguing and trying not to be overheard.

" . . . we can!" he heard Belicia say. "There is no other way."

"You would kill yourself. Let me—"

"They will destroy it. Look at what they do!"

"No statue is worth your life, my dearest Belicia."

"This one is, brother." Belicia's words shocked Slocum. He had wondered what the relationship was between bandido and *doñacita* and now he knew. He had mistaken El Jéfe's protectiveness for that of a man for his woman. A brother had been protecting his sister. Slocum closed his eyes and tried to remember everything that had happened outside Monterrey, before the robbery. Belicia had never taken part in the whoring. She might have brought the women from town, but he had never seen her with any of the soldiers.

He'd thought she had slept with El Jéfe, but he had not known the details. Belicia had stayed with her brother, probably to prevent trouble. A drunken soldier, overly amorous and not inclined to reason, would have ruined their plan. By appearing to be his woman, she had avoided much trouble.

And it had caused Slocum considerable heartache. She had single-mindedly gone after the religious statue and had never answered him directly. To her the relic was worth any risk, and her brother had aided her. But how had the son of a wealthy landowner come to be the leader of the Estrada Gang? For that Slocum would have to go to the source and ask.

Moving as quietly as he could through the tangled underbrush, he made his way up the slope until be looked down on two shadowy figures. One had a rifle thrust in front of him, aimed deeper into the canyon. Slocum couldn't see the intended target, but the boisterous laughter now echoing back told him El Jéfe had known exactly what he was doing when he'd gone after the Hughes Bunch.

Slocum jumped when a gunshot split the still of the night. Down the canyon a coyote howled in protest. Near Slocum's elbow a rabbit scurried away from its burrow; he hadn't even noticed it there until the gunshot echoed.

He lifted himself on his elbows and looked at El Jéfe to see if the man had fired. Both the bandido and his sister had dropped down. Whoever had fired was in the Hughes Bunch's camp. Slocum wasn't sure what to make of that. He edged closer to El Jéfe to overhear what he and Belicia said.

"They will destroy it!" Belicia protested. "What swine! See how they blaspheme!"

Slocum was able to look past the two and into the Hughes Bunch's camp. Curly Bill had put the Virgin Mary against a tree and was balancing pine cones on the statue's head. He'd step back a few paces, then turn and draw, firing at the pine cones. Three times he repeated it and three times the pine cones exploded. His speed and aim were deadly.

"I tell you, I could take Earp. That bag of wind couldn't stand against me. I'll do this to him!" Curly Bill fired again, this time sending his bullet ripping through the statue's middle. Wooden splinters flew everywhere and the relic toppled to one side.

El Jéfe put his hand over Belicia's mouth to keep her from crying out. Slocum moved even closer, not showing himself to either El Jéfe or the Hughes Bunch. He wasn't sure how he would be received by one, and the other would put him on the ground next to the statue in less than a heartbeat.

"Don't go drawing attention to us, Bill," Hughes warned his hotheaded friend. "We'll be in Silver City in a day or two. You can blow off steam then."

"I want Wyatt Earp," Curly Bill said. "His scalp'll hang from my belt. You wait and see."

" 'Course it will, Bill. Why not come over here and tell me how you're gonna do it?" Hughes invited, cooling off Curly Bill's fiery temper.

Slocum turned back to El Jéfe and Belicia. He heard her say, "I can do it. Please, José, let me try. What is there to lose?"

"Your life! If they see you, they will . . . kill you," El Jéfe finished lamely. Slocum knew what the man had started to say. The Hughes Bunch would take turns raping Belicia if they caught her sneaking into their camp to steal the statue. Dying would be merciful compared to what they would do first.

"I must try. You will cover me with your rifle. If any of them discovers me, kill them. That is what you want to do, anyway."

"This is safer. We will shoot them, kill them, *then* you can retrieve the santo." El Jéfe worked to a sitting position to get a better view of the camp. Slocum saw that his argument had no effect on Belicia. She was going to try no matter what her brother said.

Slocum started toward them to offer his aid. Two guns would give the woman an even better chance of getting to the statue. But Slocum wasn't able to do more than stand when Belicia darted toward the camp. El Jéfe made a grab for her, missed, and started cursing. This caused a small stir in the camp.

"What's that?" called Hughes. "Somebody's up there, boys. I heard 'em." Burros started braying and two shadow-shrouded forms rose. Sandy King and Zwing Hunt had been sleeping. Now they were drawing their six-shooters and getting ready to defend the pack train from possible thieves. Slocum shook his head at the bad luck. If El Jéfe had held his silence, Belicia might have reached the statue and got it out without anyone seeing.

Now it was a fight to the finish.

El Jéfe started spraying lead throughout the Hughes Bunch's camp. Slocum saw that the bandido's aim was terrible. Bullets ripped through tree limbs and sent splinters and sap flying, but this did nothing to slow Hughes and the others. Doc Neal went for his rifle, and King and Hunt opened up with their six-guns. Lead crisscrossed the space between El Jéfe and the camp, but no one was hit in the barrage.

Slocum saw that his plan had been shot to hell and gone. He'd be dead in minutes if he gave supporting fire for El Jéfe. Slocum started circling, thinking he could come up on the camp from the direction of the steep canyon wall. They might not expect anyone to attack from there. This would give him ample opportunity to rescue Belicia and maybe shoot a burro or two. Dead animals couldn't carry silver. Anything left would be his to take out later, after he'd evened the score with Hughes and the other outlaws in his gang.

"Back there. I see the flash from the bastard's rifle. Get 'im. Go get 'im!" Hughes motioned for his men to attack El Jéfe's position. All but Curly Bill held back.

"We don't know how many of them's up there, Jim," complained Zwing Hunt.

"There's just the one. We can take him. Get your worthless ass up there!" Hughes turned to argue with Hunt just as El Jéfe fired again. This was his first accurate shot. It took Hughes' hat off and sent it spinning into the single large campfire blazing in the middle of their bivouac. There it caught fire and burned brightly, giving El Jéfe even better targets in the camp.

Hughes ducked and spun, almost shooting Curly Bill in the back. The gunfighter charged wildly uphill, roaring out in defiance. Even if Hughes had shot him in the back, Curly Bill wouldn't have noticed. The kill lust was on him and nothing less than death would sate him now.

El Jéfe tried to end the gunman's life time and again. He fired and fired and fired, but Curly Bill led a charmed existence. The bullets went wild and Bill roared on. Slocum judged the distance, then decided he would only risk his own life by trying to stop Curly Bill. The distance was too great for a handgun, and he didn't have a clear shot in the darkness.

He turned his attention back to the camp and saw Belicia wiggling forward in the dirt. She got to the statue of the Virgin Mary and wrapped her fingers around it. Slocum thought she would be able to drag it away without being seen. And she might have, if she had tried inching out of camp. Instead, she clutched it to her breast and stood, revealing herself to everyone.

El Jéfe's fire occupied the outlaws and gave Slocum his chance. He dashed into the clearing and dived, tackling Belicia and knocking her back to the ground. The statue slipped from her fingers and rolled away. She fought like a wildcat until Slocum whispered urgently, "Stop it! They'll see you!"

When she heard this and saw who had knocked her down, she fought twice as hard.

Slocum didn't have any choice. He swung his pistol and caught Belicia on the side of the head. She sagged, stunned but not entirely unconscious. He sat beside her, eyeing the statue. It had rolled toward the fire where Hughes' hat was now glowing embers. Slocum considered his chances of reaching the religious artifact and getting back alive with it.

"John?" she said, coming back to her senses.

"Quiet. I'm not with them and haven't been since the massacre. They tried to double-cross me," Slocum said. "I've been trying to find you and El Jéfe for the past four days."

"The statue!" Belicia tried to go after the relic, but Slocum held her back. Then he clamped his hand over her mouth to keep her quiet. She hesitated when her brother started firing even faster. She turned to look uphill to where José Salazar made his stand. He had seen her danger and had come to a decision. He was drawing the Hughes Bunch's attention to give Belicia the chance to escape.

"Look," Slocum said urgently. "Look! He's giving up his life for you."

Hughes and Curly Bill split, one going left and the other moving right. Slocum wasn't sure who it was that cut down El Jéfe. He thought it might have been Jim Hughes, but it didn't matter. From the way the Mexican bandido jerked, he was dead before he hit the ground.

"José!" Belicia sobbed.

Slocum cast a quick look at the statue, then dragged Belicia into the underbrush. Hunt and King were standing next to the relic. He could take both of them, but Doc Neal and Curly Bill would get him. Two for one might be an acceptable loss for a general in battle, but it wasn't for Slocum—not when he was the one who'd do the dying.

They'd have to get away and come back for the statue—and the silver. But most of all, they had to stay alive.

13

"The Virgin Mary!" Belicia moaned. "I've got to rescue her from those pigs." She almost twisted free of Slocum's grip. He had to stick his six-shooter back into his holster and use both hands to wrestle her to the ground before she came to her senses.

"They'll kill you, and then the statue will never get back to your village," he told her. "And do you want to join your brother? José is dead."

"You know about him," she said in a choked voice. "He was the black sheep of the family, and I never told you. How did you know?"

"No time to go into that, Belicia," he said. Slocum tugged hard on her arm and pulled her deeper into the woods. Juniper limbs swung down and cut at their faces with sharp needles, but Slocum hardly noticed. He was too intent on getting away from the Hughes Bunch's camp and finding safety. He should have brought his Winchester, but happening on El Jéfe and Belicia had startled him.

"They were shooting it to splinters. I could kill them

for that. Especially the one they call Curly Bill." Belicia
clenched her hands into tight fists and ground her teeth
together until Slocum wondered if she'd have any left in
her head.

"I saw. There was nothing I could do about it. You should
have listened to José and not gone thrashing around like that.
You made it damned near impossible to ever get your santo
back. Hughes will be waiting for us to try."

Slocum didn't tell her they'd be lucky just to survive the
night. Five killers on their heels didn't make the future look
too bright. Slocum knew how to lay misleading trails, double
back and do the things necessary to make any posse lose him,
but they didn't have enough of a head start to spend much
time obliterating their tracks or even decoying Hughes and
the others.

He felt the silver slipping through his fingers. If he had
found Belicia and her brother a few minutes earlier, they
could have taken the lot of them by teaming up. El Jéfe could
have winged one or two; Slocum's more accurate marksman-
ship could have accounted for three. All that silver, just his,
El Jéfe's and Belicia's. A ton of silver apiece. Not even
Crocker or Stanford could match a fortune like that.

"I hear them behind us. They are like bulls charging
through the woods," Belicia said.

"They're herding us. Doc Neal and Hughes might have
been able to circle and get between us and the horses. We're
probably walking straight into a trap." Slocum clutched
his pistol even tighter and got ready for the shootout. It
had to come soon, but it got on his nerves not knowing
exactly when.

A head popped up unexpectedly off to Slocum's right. He
whirled, aimed and fired in one smooth motion. A hat spun
off into the brush, and Slocum knew he had been suckered.
Someone had put a skunk cabbage on the end of a stick and
stuck his hat on it to draw fire. Slocum had revealed their
location and gained nothing in return.

"Back," he said suddenly. "Double back and move to the

left. We've got to get out of here."

"But our horses are over there."

Slocum jerked the woman's hand down and tackled her just as a ragged volley echoed through the woods. The bullets ripped foliage from the shrubs around them. Slocum painfully moved off Belicia, wincing at the tiny cuts he'd gotten from the blackberry bush's sharp, short thorns. He pushed the woman ahead of him even as the line of bullets came closer and closer.

"They're close by, men," Hughes called. "I think I hit Slocum. The son of a bitch isn't going to double-cross us!"

"So," Belicia said, "It is true. You are not with them."

"Glad you finally figured that out," Slocum said sarcastically. He didn't have time for anything but staying alive, and he wasn't exactly sure how he was going to do it.

"What did you do? Try to steal the silver from them?"

"I complained about butchering the Estradas," he said. "I can't seem to keep from making the same mistake over and over." He didn't explain to her how Quantrill had gut-shot him for complaining about the slaughter of innocent women and children during the Lawrence, Kansas raid during the war. Quantrill, Bloody Bill Anderson and the others had given no quarter, whether to soldier or civilian. Slocum's complaint had left him an invalid for almost a year, and he had repeated the mistake with Jim Hughes.

With men like that, it never did to protest their brutality.

More bullets ripped through the air just over Slocum's head. He let out a long, anguished cry that startled Belicia. He clamped his hand over her mouth and whispered, "Play along with it. I want them to think they hit me."

"Careful, Hunt," came Hughes' warning. "He's a sneaky one. He might be laying a trap."

"I hit 'im, Jim. I know I did."

Slocum knew he wouldn't get a second shot. When Zwing Hunt's dark shape appeared outlined against lighter foliage Slocum fired. He cursed himself because he knew he'd missed. He might have grazed Hunt, but he'd never bet real money on it. There hadn't been a shout of outrage or a moan of pain. There was . . . nothing.

Slocum pointed in the direction they had been traveling. Belicia hurried ahead while Slocum moved slower to see if she flushed any of the Hughes Bunch. He heard nothing, and this worried him. They hadn't given up and his tiny ruse hadn't worked. Hughes was too crafty for that, but it never hurt to try.

Slocum circled the outlaws, trying to get to the side and catch them by surprise. He got off another shot but didn't come within a country mile of doing any damage. Belicia came up beside him. They were cut off from their horses, and Slocum heard burros braying a hundred yards off. He still intended to kill as many of the burros as he could to force the Hughes Bunch into abandoning some of the silver.

More important now was just staying alive. Slocum pushed Belicia down and let two men pass within ten feet. He couldn't tell who they were but thought it was Doc Neal and Curly Bill.

"What happened to them, Jim?" one man called. "It's just like the earth opened up and swallowed them."

"Keep your tater trap shut, King," snapped Hughes. "They'll get away for sure if you go making too much noise."

Slocum knew they were all blundering around in the dark woods, not sure where anyone else was. As hard as it was for Belicia, he forced her to just sit still. The longer the outlaws roamed the woods, the edgier they got and the more likely they were to kill each other. Slocum kept a sharp eye out for a good shot, but nothing came. The search for them had drifted farther toward the canyon wall.

This presented a dilemma for him. They might be able to reach their horses now, but did he want to? Leaving behind his share of the silver rankled like a burr under a saddle blanket. That money was *his*.

"We can go into their camp," Belicia said. "There might be something for each of us there." She had been reading his expression accurately. And her words decided for him.

"The horses," he said. "We should get the hell out of here. Hughes might be setting a trap for us, expecting us to go nosing around the camp. It's better to run, let them get careless in a day or two and then we'll take what we want." Even as he spoke Slocum knew what he'd really do. He'd see Belicia to safety and then ride straight back to fetch his share of the Monterrey silver.

"Very well," she said, not giving him any argument. He stopped and just stared at her. This wasn't like her, and he suspected some small treachery. But Belicia made a beeline for the horses. He held her back for several minutes while he did some scouting, wary of a trap. Hughes hadn't found the horses. Slocum waved Belicia to her horse. They mounted and rode slowly away, trying to keep their animals quiet. A half mile up the canyon, Slocum said, "We ought to put all the distance between them and us we can."

"You want me to ride ahead?" Her dark eyes caught the moon and shone like the silver Slocum hungered after.

"Go on. My horse is tired. There's no reason—"

"You want to take them on single-handedly. José tried that and failed. Do not do it, John. For my sake. For your own."

She sounded sincere, but Slocum knew the fire burning in her breast would never die. She wanted the santo and wasn't going to be talked out of it any more than he'd be talked out of getting his share from the robbery.

"You know me too well. And I know you, too, Belicia. Let's ride a ways farther, then rest. We can wait a day or two, lull them into thinking we're gone, then do what has to be done." He watched to see if this carried any weight with her. The logic of it seemed enough for the moment. She nodded slowly, and he wasn't sure she knew he could see the motion in the darkness.

"We have no other choice. They are five to our two, and they have weapons."

"And ammo," Slocum added. He had a few dozen rounds left, for both his Colt and his rifle. That wouldn't let him get into any protracted gunfight. Whatever they did to get the silver and statue would have to be done by stealth rather than a frontal assault.

They rode in silence. Slocum made them zigzag back and forth, cross streams, double back for a few minutes, then cut across their old trail to confuse anyone trying to track them at daybreak. It would take a tracker as good as Slocum himself to find them, and Slocum doubted any of the Hughes Bunch wanted to spend the tedious hours on hands and knees deciphering the spoor.

After an hour, Slocum called a halt to their flight. He didn't want to put too much distance between them and the pack train. He needed to catch up quickly when the time was right. It would be a balancing act keeping far enough back to avoid detection and yet near enough for the final swoop down, the quick theft of the statue and silver, and the getaway.

"We've got a stream nearby and the horses have plenty of grass," he said. "We can bed down over there among the tree roots. That'll protect us if anybody tries sneaking up on us."

"What?" she asked in mock horror. "No all-night watch? No guard duty to keep us secure?"

Slocum had to laugh at her mocking tone. He had been far too serious. She knew what had to be done.

"We're both too tired to waste precious time listening to owls and the burble of the stream. Our time's better spent sleeping."

"You are a strange man, John Slocum," she said. "You risked your life for me and José when there was no need. The mob in Monterrey would have trapped us for certain, yet you helped us escape. Why is that?"

Slocum didn't have a good answer. He had been wrong so often about her that he wasn't sure what he had been thinking at the time. Belicia was more positive about what she wanted, and it wasn't sleep. She came to him and knelt. Her hand reached out and touched his cheek, moved back and through his lank black hair. She pressed her fingers into the back of his neck and drew him forward slightly.

Slocum wasn't going to deny her what he wanted also, but it was going to be his doing. His arms circled her and pulled the woman close. She seemed to melt in his grasp. Their lips crushed together. Belicia's hands stroked through Slocum's hair as he kissed her fiercely. All the tension bottled within him seemed to rush out, electrifying both of them.

"I want you so," Slocum whispered hotly in her ear when he broke off the kiss. "I thought you were El Jéfe's woman."

"But he was—" Belicia lurched back, startled. Then she laughed. "I see how it must have looked. José was always a renegade. He and my father never agreed. José thought he could rule all Mexico one day."

"And you wanted only to return a religious relic to your people," Slocum said. He fingered the buttons on Belicia's blouse, teasing them open one at a time. When he pulled open the blouse and exposed her firm, brown breasts he saw the nipples were already as hard as the buttons. He toyed with them and made her moan softly.

"Yes," she sighed, pressing closer so that her breasts flattened in his hands. He bent forward and kissed each nipple, first the left and then the right, returning to the left to suckle. Belicia shivered all over and sank to the ground.

He wasn't sure what she was saying yes to and it hardly mattered. Her hands worked to free him of his gunbelt and trousers, even as he slid his hands down her flanks, down her legs and to bare skin. Then he moved upward again, under her skirt until he touched the furred triangle between her thighs.

A new shudder passed through her, more intense, more demanding than before. She pulled him down and whispered hotly in his ear, "Make love to me. Take me. I am yours, John, all yours!"

He grew harder by the second. Her slender thighs parted willingly for him as he moved into the cradle of her hips. Her knees rose and allowed him easier entry. For a moment, he paused, the tip of his manhood resting against the dampness of her nether lips. They both savored the moment and then Slocum couldn't wait any longer. With a long, smooth motion, he levered his hips forward and sank to the hilt into the woman's clutching interior.

"You're so much for me, John. So big." Belicia moaned softly but her fingers tore at his back. Slocum tried to keep his movement slow, sure, and pleasurable for both of them, but he felt the fire burning in his loins. He could hardly hold back. Everything he had thought of Belicia was wrong. She could be his.

She was his now.

He pulled back and hesitated only an instant before thrusting back. Once more he was surrounded by clinging warm female flesh. He started moving in the ages old rhythm of a man loving a woman, and Belicia responded fully. Her hips rose off the ground to meet his every inward thrust. She even twisted and turned slightly to give him more stimulation. And Slocum wasn't sure how she did it but every stroke found her tighter than the previous one. She was crushing him as if she gripped down with a firm velvet glove. And Slocum moved even faster, his hips flying now as the fiery tide rose within him.

The woman shrieked, then bit her lower lip to keep from crying out even more. The sound triggered the explosion lurking inside Slocum. He erupted into her hungry womb. They rocked together, locked at the groin, and then the passion slipped away from both of them. Spent, they lay in each other's arms.

Belicia lightly kissed him and then she fell asleep. Slocum took longer to find real rest. He lay awake for almost an hour, staring at the stars and wondering what was going to happen. Belicia was one in a million, but he might have to give her up if he wanted to get any of the silver.

Was any woman worth a half ton of silver? He pulled her closer and she snuggled in the hollow of his shoulder, her warm breath gusting lightly against his flesh. If any woman was, it just might be Belicia Salazar.

14

The pounding of horses' hooves awoke Slocum just after dawn. He pushed free of Belicia's arms and rolled to his feet, getting into his trousers as he went. He grabbed his six-shooter, not bothering to put on the gunbelt. Before he had pulled on his boots, the horses thundered past.

He watched in amazement as the cavalry troop passed within twenty yards, oblivious to Slocum and Belicia. The troopers had the weary look of men who had been in the saddle too long, never quite getting enough sleep when they did bivouac. Their leader, a shavetail lieutenant who might not even be able to grow a decent beard yet, rode at attention, his back ramrod straight and his eyes determinedly forward. This military posture was all that saved Slocum from discovery.

None of the troopers was interested in anything but riding, and their lieutenant was fixed on some destination to the north. His head was high and his chin thrust forward as if begging someone to clip him one. Before the last of the column passed, Belicia was awake and dressing.

"The horses," he whispered. "They will give us away."

Slocum heard the two animals whinnying and snorting. His chestnut began pawing the ground and tugging hard at her reins. He hurried to soothe them. His mare quieted easily but Belicia's mount refused to quiet. It reared, threatening him with viciously flailing front hooves.

"I will gentle my horse," Belicia said. She pushed past Slocum and began calling to the horse in a soothing voice. Slocum didn't know which would be worse. Belicia's voice carried on the still morning air, but the noise made by the horse might draw more attention. The column of troopers was after someone and Slocum had the gut feeling it might be the Hughes Bunch. If so, the lieutenant would investigate any unusual sound.

"There, there," Belicia said, finally calming the horse. "We are ready to ride. Where do we go? How will we even the score with Hughes?"

Slocum didn't have an easy answer for that. If El Jéfe had somehow alerted the cavalry to Hughes' presence, all the silver might be lost. It would be the ultimate revenge for the Mexican bandido, but it would leave Slocum without anything to show for his part in the robbery. Simply keeping Hughes and the others from enjoying their take wasn't enough.

Slocum wanted a few hundred pounds of the precious metal for his own. He'd earned it.

"Shadowing the pack train might be good enough," Slocum said, thinking aloud. "I can shoot a few of the burros and make them leave that silver behind. They might get the notion that it's to pay me off and not raise any more ruckus."

"But the Virgin Mary!" protested Belicia. "There is no guarantee they will abandon the santo when they leave behind your silver. And José screams for revenge from his grave!"

"What grave?" Slocum asked harshly. José Salazar hadn't received a Christian burial. Hughes would have left the bandido's body out for the buzzards to pick clean.

"All the more reason to make Hughes pay for what he has done. He has defiled my family's name. He has stolen a religious relic belonging to my village. He has killed my brother. And he has double-crossed you and stolen your silver." Belicia added the last reason to give Slocum a stake in recovering her precious statue. He didn't rise to the bait. He knew all the arguments for killing Jim Hughes.

"We'll track them and let them fall into believing we've left them alone. We may be dead for all they'll know."

"But what of the cavalry?" Belicia asked. "Are they not on Hughes' trail, also?"

Slocum worried about that. The column had been in a hurry, and it was going in roughly the same direction taken by the Hughes Bunch and their pack train. In the winding canyons of the Peloncillo Mountains, though, there were few choices. Many canyons were deadends and others didn't provide a passage to anywhere important. To the north lay Silver City and to the east were a half-dozen small towns Slocum couldn't even remember. If the soldiers headed in either direction, they had to pass this way.

They rode silently while the sun crept up the sky. The day turned hot, in spite of the coolness offered by the trees and occasional streams that bubbled along before vanishing at the edge of the Sonora Desert. Slocum let his eyes close as a breeze blew into his face. He drifted along half-asleep, mesmerized by the distant sound of birds.

His eyes shot open when the bird calls stopped. He reined back and blinked hard, letting his eyes adjust to the brightness of the sun. He called out to Belicia.

"What is it, John?"

"Birds. Listen."

"There are none. So?"

"There were a few seconds ago. Something ahead disturbed them." He tried to penetrate the thick stand of juniper and scrub oak but saw nothing except dark shadows. The trail meandered through the woods. To leave it and go higher into the rocks along the canyon face would waste precious time. Slocum was sure the Hughes Bunch had come this way, and so had the cavalry troopers.

"It's a trap," he said. "I don't know who's laying it, but we're goners if we ride into that stand." He pulled his rifle from its saddle sheath and jacked a round into the chamber.

"How can you be so sure?" She looked apprehensive but not unduly frightened. "I see and hear nothing."

"That's the problem. *All* animal sounds are gone. Something's spooked them into silence." He studied the route along the cliff face and didn't like it. They'd be exposed there, sitting ducks for any marksman down in the wooded patch.

"It might be the noise of Hughes' passage. So many braying burros would—" Belicia bit back her words. Slight movement alerted her to the danger.

"Apaches," Slocum said. "Back. Back along the trail and hope they don't come for us!" He wheeled his chestnut mare around and put his heels to the animal's sides. The horse was tired but responded with a surge of speed that almost took Slocum out of the saddle. He bent forward, hoping the Apaches were after other prey.

The whoops from behind told him they had not only seen him and Belicia but were giving chase.

"What are we to do?" gasped Belicia, riding leg to leg with Slocum. Her horse was tiring by the second. Slocum's wasn't in much better condition. Galloping for even a mile would kill both horses.

"Ride upslope," he called out. "We can make a stand there." Slocum didn't have much hope that they'd be able to sidestep the Apaches, or outfight them if the Indians decided on coming after their scalps, but he'd put up one hell of a fight first.

The loose gravel made the going even harder for the horses, but they got to a ragged trail above the canyon bottom. Slocum dismounted and swung his rifle around to cover the slope. He could potshot anyone trying to come after them. But there weren't any Apaches in sight.

"We have outrun them," Belicia said with a sigh of relief. "Where does this trail lead?"

"To the canyon rim, unless I miss my guess," Slocum said. "And I don't think we've outrun them, or outsmarted them. Start walking the horses. I'll cover your retreat."

"But, John, there is no reason."

"Do it!" Slocum was in no mood to argue. He had a bad feeling that they were in as much trouble as before. Along this stony ledge they couldn't dodge fire and were sitting ducks for anyone hiding below. Belicia took his horse's reins and tugged gently, getting the mare to move without shying. Slocum waited a few minutes, then trailed her warily looking all around. He saw nothing and this made him even edgier.

The trail rose steeply, going toward the canyon rim as he had guessed. Belicia and the horses vanished over the top. Slocum started up the last few feet, looked up at the sky, and was suddenly set upon by a flying Apache. The Indian had risen up from just over the rise and launched himself at Slocum.

Slocum's lightning reflexes kept the Indian's knife from gutting him. He threw up his rifle like a quarterstaff and knocked the blade to one side, but the weight of the Indian's body hit Slocum full force and sent him tumbling back down the slope. Razor sharp bits of flint slashed at his back, but Slocum didn't notice as he slid backward, kicking hard at the Indian who was trying to pin him to the ground and make another cut with his knife.

Locking one hand around the Apache's wrist, Slocum twisted to the side and tried to dislodge his attacker. The Apache was too strong for that. Powerful legs clamped Slocum's body in a viselike grip and the Indian's other hand sought Slocum's exposed throat.

Screaming at the top of his lungs gave Slocum just enough power to fling the Indian in the other direction from his first attempt at escape. The Apache rocked and Slocum; got enough leverage to heave even harder. The Indian tried to force himself forward and pin Slocum's shoulder; this was his undoing. Slocum relaxed and used the slope to his advantage. The Apache tumbled over to land downhill with a hard thud.

Like a snake, Slocum whipped around, got to his feet and swung as hard as he could. He caught the Indian square on the jaw. The shock rolled up Slocum's arm and exploded in his shoulder like thunder, deadening the nerves. But the blow lifted the Apache off his feet and sent him sliding down the hill on his back, unconscious. Slocum rubbed his bruised knuckles and made his way back up the hill, not knowing what he'd find.

"Aieee!"

Slocum's world was suddenly filled with another attacking Indian. Slocum went for his Colt Navy but his bruised hand was too cramped for his usual swift draw. He fumbled and felt strong arms circling his body like steel bands. He spun and lifted the Indian off the ground. Slocum landed heavily atop the Apache, one knee in the other's groin. The Indian shrieked in agony and gave Slocum the chance to stumble away, trying to regain his equilibrium.

"John, look out!" came Belicia's warning. Slocum ducked just as another Apache attacked him, his silver knife flashing. A rifle shot rang out and the Indian toppled over the rim and slid down the hill to join his still unconscious kindred.

Slocum saw Belicia fighting for her life with another Indian. This time he was able to draw and used both hands to steady his Colt. The single shot took the Apache in the back. The Indian sank to the ground without uttering a word.

"Who shot the other one?" Slocum demanded. He spun, pistol ready. He heard the clank of harness and the shouted commands of a cavalry officer. He dropped to his belly and scooted forward to look over the rise. Somehow the young lieutenant and a half dozen of his column had followed along the stony ledge and had come up just in time to shoot the Apache attacking Slocum. Whether he had seen Slocum was a moot point. He was blocking escape down that trail. The only way open for deliverance was along the exposed, rocky canyon rim.

The officer stopped to look at the Indian Slocum had cold-cocked, but there wouldn't be much time before he rode on up to the rim. Slocum didn't have any desire to spend the rest of his day explaining to the lieutenant why he and Belicia were here. Worse, the officer might be on patrol to find the Hughes Bunch.

The payroll robbery had only happened a few weeks earlier and was especially bloody. The U.S. Army wasn't likely to let that crime be forgotten any time soon. With as many wanted posters on him as there were, Slocum didn't dare let the officer drag him back to some distant fort for questioning.

"We ride, Belicia," he said, running to his horse and vaulting into the saddle. "We ride and we try not to get caught."

How they were going to do that on exhausted horses was something he didn't want to think about too much.

15

"I cannot ride any more," Belicia said, fatigue etching her lovely face. She slumped forward and almost fell off the horse. Slocum wanted to keep going. The cavalry couldn't be too far behind, but he knew they had to rest. If they pushed the horses any more, the animals would die under them and leave them stranded.

"All right," he said, seeing a secluded area down the canyon where they had fled. The cavalry lieutenant might not have come after them, sticking only to the canyon rim for his patrol. He might have been green enough to think he'd tangled with only a few Apaches and never noticed the tracks left by shod horses. Or he might not have cared. His mission might have been nothing more than to kill redskins escaped from their reservation.

"Are they after us?" Belicia asked, dismounting and walking her horse. The animal stumbled repeatedly from tiredness. Slocum cursed when he saw this. Even without a rider, the horse couldn't continue without running the chance of

125

dying. They might have to hole up here a day or more.
That increased the risk of being discovered by the cavalry
detachment, or Apaches.

Worse than this, the Hughes Bunch would keep a steady
pace with their string of burros and be days down the road.
Slocum was sure he could trail them, given time. The ground
was rocky and he didn't know the terrain, but thirty burros
left a hell of a trail behind. Unless Jim Hughes got suspicious or the cavalry spooked him, he wouldn't try to cover
his spoor.

"I don't know. I ought to check," Slocum said. He dismounted, also, and let his chestnut mare have her head. The
weary horse walked with a surer gait than her companion but
there wasn't the old spring and prance to the step. Slocum
resigned himself to camping at least overnight and maybe
into the next day.

Hughes and the silver would have to wait. Slocum's only
consolation was knowing even an outlaw like Jim Hughes
couldn't spend that much silver in a day or a week or even
a month.

"I am as tired as my horse," Belicia said. She took her
blanket and curled up under a tree, head resting against a
gnarled root. Slocum watched her for a few minutes. She
fell asleep almost instantly. Slocum tended the horses, saw
that they had enough water but not so much that they bloated,
then staked them near the stream where they could rest and
graze on a patch of grass. Bone-tired himself, he still had
to be sure they were safe.

He took his Winchester and hiked back along their trail,
climbing onto a boulder and squinting into the distance. He
could see almost a mile of the winding canyon behind them.
He waited for more than an hour, alert for any sign that the
troopers had followed them. When he saw nothing out of the
ordinary, he began to relax. He had been overly suspicious,
too cautious, not willing to take the risk required to recover
his silver. There weren't any Indians or cavalry unit after
him, nothing but ghosts. He sat and stared into the distance

and his eyes slowly lost focus. He stretched out on the rock like a lizard in the sun and was asleep in a few minutes.

"The horse does not limp as badly now, John," Belicia pointed out. They had been walking her horse the better part of two days, making only a few miles in the winding canyons before having to camp for the night. Slocum chafed at the delay. Every passing minute put that much more distance between the Hughes Bunch and the muzzle of his Colt Navy. Still, there was no way to hurry healing. Belicia's horse had pulled up lame the day after the cavalry had saved his neck from the Apaches.

"You might cause the horse to stumble if the leg's not ready to support a rider," Slocum said. Good sense spoke, but he wanted to agree with Belicia and tell her to mount. He wanted to gallop, to race the wind through the canyons.

"I want the statue," she said, suddenly changing the subject. "I want it more than you do the silver. The Virgin Mary is more than simple worldly riches. We need riches of the soul more."

His own thoughts had been on the silver. They hadn't been making good time, but he worried that they hadn't crossed Hughes' trail. He had been watching carefully and ought to have seen some sign of the Hughes Bunch or the thirty burros, some evidence that another human had passed this way in the last few days.

There had been nothing. Nothing at all.

"We're not going to find anything unless we travel faster and farther," Slocum said. He didn't want to abandon Belicia in the mountains with a lame horse, but he could ride faster alone and find Hughes.

"How would you ever find me again? I will *not* let the Virgin Mary stay in that pig's hands." Belicia stamped her foot and the set to her jaw told Slocum he wouldn't be able to simply ride off without a hell of a fight on his hands. He and Belicia were partners in the revenge against the Hughes Bunch and the recovery of both silver and statue.

"We'll find them," he said, letting out a sigh of exasperation. He felt the haul from the Monterrey mint slipping further away. Why hadn't he found Hughes' trail? He had gone up one canyon and down another. There weren't that many possibilities, unless Hughes had radically altered his path and found one of the smaller, winding canyons to go north.

Slocum sighed again. He wasn't even sure Hughes was headed north. The outlaws had told him they were going to Silver City, but that might have been a lie. Slocum dropped to a squatting position beside a tiny pool of water, ladled a few drops to his lips, and thought hard on this. Hughes wasn't the only one who had told him they were going to Silver City. Curly Bill was too arrogant and sure of his gun-handling ability to lie. If anything, he'd want to face Slocum in a shootout. Any man fool enough to think he could take Wyatt Earp in a fair fight was too stupid to lie.

"You are thinking as I am," Belicia said. "They have gone to Silver City. I heard them talking often of this town. Is it far?"

"With your horse like it is, we're a week or more away. And there's no reason to think they really wanted to head there."

"John, John," Belicia chided. "They spoke when they did not think I overheard. They were going to Silver City. What other choice do we have?"

"None," Slocum said, rising and rubbing his damp hands across his face. He decided they could make better time if they both rode his horse and walked Belicia's. They might not make as many miles in a day as he'd have liked, but they'd get to Silver City faster. Somehow, that seemed to matter more and more to him.

They'd shot Belicia's horse two days earlier when it stumbled and stepped into a rabbit's burrow. Slocum wasn't sure the horse had broken its leg, but it had severely damaged the leg it had been hobbling on for almost a week. There was

no other way to ease its obvious misery. He was as glad to
see a small town as he had ever been when they rode into
Silver City.

The sleepy little town had once boomed with silver mines
in the mountains surrounding it, but now all that was mined
was copper along with an occasional vein of coal. Slocum
dismounted and let Belicia remain on the tired chestnut's
back. Slocum patted his horse's neck and said softly, "Grain.
You get all the grain you can eat for this." The horse turned
a huge brown eye toward him and whinnied, as if telling
him she'd believe it when she saw it.

"Let's hitch up there," Slocum said, pointing to a post
outside a saloon. He had a thirst so big he could drop a dust
devil into it. He took one step up onto the boardwalk and
then stopped. Belicia couldn't join him, not here. There'd
be talk enough about a Mexican woman riding into town
with a white man. To take her into a saloon would brand
her a whore.

"John, look. At the end of the street." Belicia's voice was
small, choked, barely audible.

He turned and looked in the direction she indicated, not
sure what he saw. His hand drifted toward his Colt, but he
didn't draw. There was no need.

"Damnation," he swore. "We're too late."

"Let's find out what happened," she said, slipping from
the saddle. Belicia walked toward the crude gallows like one
condemned. She watched the slow swinging of the man—
his neck stretched by the hangman's noose—almost as if
she was the next to be executed.

"You know that owlhoot?" came a cold voice from the
shadows. Slocum didn't turn and draw but it took all his
will power not to. Only one man in town would be asking
a question like that in the knife-edged tone.

"Reckon I might, Sheriff," Slocum answered. "That's Jim
Hughes, isn't it?"

"We strung him up a bit past noon today. How do you
come to know him, you and the lady?" The lawman moved

into the light cast from the open doors leading into the saloon. He was a big man who radiated authority. He wore a small caliber pistol stuck into his belt, but Slocum wasn't about to challenge him. He didn't doubt that the sheriff could pull the .32 and get off a couple rounds in the time it took most men just to touch the handles of their hoglegs.

"He robbed us out on the trail. The cavalry was looking for him. Stole the lady's horse maybe a week back. You see the troopers?"

"Can't say I did," the lawman allowed.

"Some young lieutenant was at the head of the column," Belicia said, smiling sweetly. The lawman's coldness melted just a mite at the show of friendliness.

"The army don't stop much in these parts," the sheriff said. "They don't have a call to 'cuz I keep the peace."

"I can see," Slocum said, watching in grim fascination as the wind whipping down from the White Mountains made Hughes' body spin slowly. The black bag was still around the outlaw's head and his hands were tied behind him, but Slocum recognized the leader of the Hughes Bunch.

"It is not enough," Belicia said suddenly. "There should have been more."

"What you talkin' about?" the sheriff asked.

"He stole my horse. He should have been forced to return it before you hung him."

"The horse he rode looked like it was his. Him and the others didn't have any spares with them."

Slocum wanted to ask about a pack train of thirty burros but refrained. Too many questions would make the already suspicious lawman go leafing through stacks of wanted posters stuffed into a drawer back in his office. All it took was for the sheriff to find one on Slocum to bring down a peck of trouble.

"My horse," grumbled Belicia, getting into the play-acting. "There were others with him?" She pointed to the grisly sight on the gallows.

The sheriff laughed without humor. "More of them bastards? Excuse me, ma'am. Surely were more of them. Four others. They got what was coming to them for all they did."

Slocum touched Belicia's arm to signal her to stop pumping the lawman for information. Anything that got Hughes hanged would be the talk of the town. They could find out everything they needed to know without arousing the sheriff's curiosity.

"Don't reckon we'll see the horse again," Slocum said. "It was a strong pony, about eight-hands high. Had two white stockings and—"

"Haven't seen any horse like that," the sheriff said. "I'll keep an eye out. If anybody turns up riding it, I might get me another one to hang alongside this one." The sheriff touched the brim of his hat, gave Belicia a last appreciative look and sauntered off in the direction of the saloon where a fight had erupted. One man crashed through the front door and landed in the street, another following him.

"What are we to do, John?" Belicia chewed her lower lip in worry and wrung her hands as if they hurt.

"Ask around and find out what happened to the other four. If Hughes got his neck stretched, the others might be dead."

"The santo," Belicia moaned. "It might be lost forever."

Slocum said nothing about it or the silver. Hughes wouldn't have ridden into Silver City with the take from Monterrey. He must have hidden it sometime during the last week. But where? The mountains had more places to stash three tons of silver than he could shake a stick at. Losing the Hughes Bunch's trail had been a minor setback, or so he'd thought.

Now he cursed himself for not being better, for not looking closer and finding it, of giving up too easily. The others in the gang had to be alive. They had to be so Slocum could wring out the silver's hiding place from them.

"There's where we do some shopping," Slocum said. He pointed to the general store. An old man sat out front, whittling half-heartedly at a stick of pine. A pile of shavings circled his chair. "Go inside and get what we might need out on the trail. I'll find out what I can from him."

Belicia nodded and entered the store. Slocum saw that they had little time. It was dusk and the town was closing up, except the saloon which would get noisier until the sheriff shut it down or went in and joined the revelers himself.

"Evening," Slocum said, nodding toward the old man who looked up with rheumy eyes.

"Don't think I know you. You just blow into town?"

"Did," Slocum said, sitting on the edge of the walk. "The lady and I are heading on out of town as soon as we can find a horse for her. Nothing too expensive."

"What happened to her horse?"

This was the opening Slocum needed to launch into his lie about Hughes stealing Belicia's horse. He worked around, getting names and prices of anyone in town willing to sell a horse as he pieced together all that had happened the past two days in Silver City.

"Don't get excitement like that, no sir," the old man said. He turned and spat into the dirt. A large black gob of mud showed how long he had been sitting on the porch. "They rode in as bold as brass yesterday morning. And then all hell was out for lunch. Yes sir, that's the way it was."

Slocum kept prodding and got the full story after a spell. Doc Neal had got drunk and started bragging about how rich he was. He'd flashed a considerable pouch of Mexican coins and had drawn attention to himself when he bought drinks for everyone. An Easterner, a greenhorn from the old man's account, had taken an interest in the coins and had been more than a tad insistent on finding out their source.

Jim Hughes had gunned the Easterner down and that started the bloodshed.

A posse had chased the Hughes Bunch out of town and Doc Neal had been cut down less than a mile from where Jim

Hughes swung in the wind. Curly Bill and Sandy King had gotten clean away and Zwing Hunt had been captured.

"So why didn't they hang this Hunt fellow, too?" Slocum asked.

"Didn't have much on him. He never drew his six-shooter and mostly he sat around drunker'n a lord when all the gunplay was happening," the old man said. "They wanted to jug him for something, though, so he got thirty days for drunk and disorderly."

"They hung Hughes but gave Hunt thirty days for not doing anything more than getting drunk?" Slocum shook his head. He might live to be a hundred years old and he'd never figure out how the law worked. Zwing Hunt was as guilty as Hughes of a dozen crimes, yet Hughes was hanged and Hunt was doing time for having a few drinks too many.

As bizarre as it seemed to him, he knew Lady Luck was finally smiling on him. Tracking Curly Bill and Sandy King would be hard. Jim Hughes was dead, as was Doc Neal. But Zwing Hunt could tell him where they'd stashed the silver. Slocum's fingers slipped back and forth over the worn smoothness of his six-shooter's ebony handle. Hunt would tell him everything he needed to know. Everything.

"Yep, they got him locked up over in the jailhouse," the old man said, working on the slip of pine until he had nothing but a toothpick left. He reached over, picked up another piece, and started turning it into shavings. "You a friend of his?" The man cocked his head to one side and studied Slocum carefully.

"No friend. He rode with that one, the horse thief."

"Whatever you say, mister," the old man replied, a slight smile on his lips. Slocum nodded and went to see what Belicia had bought. They didn't have much money between them, but the information was worth more than the cost of salt pork and beans.

He almost ran into Belicia as she hurried from the store, a wrapped package under her arm. She glanced in the whittling man's direction, then indicated she had to speak with Slocum out of the old geezer's hearing. Slocum knew that might be at the far end of the street. From his post in front of the general store, not much would get by the old man.

Slocum guided Belicia away, aware that the old man watched them like a hawk as they marched off. Belicia kept trying to tell him what she had discovered and Slocum kept hushing her. He didn't let her tell him the same details he had found out until they were at the edge of town and away from all Silver City's residents.

"One is in *jail*," Belicia exclaimed. "It is Hunt. I never liked him. He has shifty eyes."

"I found that out, too," Slocum said. "We've got to get a horse for you, then see if we can find out what they did with the silver."

"And the Virgin Mary," Belicia said firmly.

Slocum nodded. And the statue. But first, he'd squeeze from Hunt what the Hughes Bunch had done with thirty burros laden with Monterrey silver. With Doc Neal and Hughes dead, that left only three in the gang. A four-way split would be nice, Slocum decided, but keeping three tons of silver all for himself would be even better.

After all, he had earned it when Hughes tried the double-cross.

Three tons of silver. More wealth than he'd ever dreamed of possessing. Half-a-million dollars. And it would be his, by damn, it would!

16

"There is no way you can do it," Belicia protested. "The sheriff is already suspicious of us. I knew it when we walked away."

Slocum didn't tell her the lawman was too busy watching her ass wiggle to do much hard thinking about the people claiming Hughes had stolen a horse from them. Still, she had a point. The sheriff might get downright suspicious if they asked to talk to Zwing Hunt. That meant they had to pry the information from the outlaw without anyone knowing. Slocum knew how hard that might be.

"Is there a deputy watching the cell?" he asked. They stood across the street from the jailhouse, having wasted the past two hours finding a horse. The best Slocum was able to buy was a swaybacked nag that wouldn't be able to run more than a mile before keeling over. It was hardly more than fodder for a glue factory, but Silver City didn't offer much in the way of horseflesh at the prices he could afford.

"I see only one man. He sleeps at the desk. His head rests on crossed arms. What should we do?"

135

"You watch him. If the deputy wakes up or the sheriff returns, stall them. Give them any story that comes to mind. I'll try to talk to Hunt through his cell window."

"John," Belicia said, grabbing his arm and holding it tightly. "You do not double-cross me, do you? The silver is everything for you. It is nothing to me. Keep the money. But the statue . . ." She let the sentence trail off. As he gazed into her dark brown eyes he knew he wasn't going to trade her for the silver.

"Don't rightly see why we both can't get what we want most. Zwing Hunt's liable to be a real talker by the time I'm done with him."

"Don't do anything foolish," Belicia said, standing on tiptoe and giving him a quick kiss. "We can do great things together, you and I."

"Once the santo is back in your village?" he asked. He read the answer in her expression. She would do anything to recover the statue. She wanted to be with him, but not if it meant sacrificing the religious artifact.

"Hurry," she said. "I do not like this town or the way everyone watches."

The old man in front of the general store had left, but clumps of men roamed endlessly up and down Silver City's streets. Slocum had never seen a place quite like this. Everyone walked and everyone was curious about the strangers. It might have been the way the Hughes Bunch had stirred them up two days earlier, or the hanging, or maybe it was the prospect of someone else getting his neck stretched. Whatever it was, Slocum had to agree with Belicia. The sooner they left, the better he would like it.

He walked halfway down the street, as if heading for the saloon for a drink, made sure no one was watching closely, then ducked into a dark alley and doubled back. The adobe building holding the cells was too sturdy to tunnel through. A stick of dynamite might not have done more than crack the sun-dried, mud-brick wall; but the open barred window held more promise. Slocum waited until he was sure no one saw him, then went to the first window and peered through the bars.

The cell was empty, as was the second and third. Slocum began to worry that the sheriff had lied to him, that Zwing Hunt had been cut down, too. But the last window, the corner cell, held a man snoring loudly. The thin blanket rose and fell as he breathed. Slocum climbed onto a crate and called out Hunt's name. The figure stirred, grunted and tried to roll over.

"Hunt!" To Slocum's ears the name rang out in the still night like a gunshot. The man in the cell mumbled again but didn't awaken. Slocum called out again. This time Hunt sat up and rubbed his eyes.

"How long do you want to rot in there?" Slocum asked.

"Slocum!" Hunt scrambled away from the window, hands grabbing for a pistol that wasn't stuck into his belt. He settled down and stared at Slocum, outlined in the window by the rising moon.

"I want my share of the silver," Slocum said, not bandying words. "Where did Hughes hide it?"

"I'm not going to tell you!"

Slocum whipped out his pistol and thrust it through the bars. Hunt stared down the barrel. His hands shook as he reached out, as if he could fend off a bullet.

"Don't kill me, Slocum. It's not worth it. They hung Hughes. They'll string you alongside him if you murder me."

"Don't flatter yourself. They might give me a medal for saving them the cost of feeding you for a month. Where's the silver?"

"We hid it. In an old mine shaft."

Slocum sucked in a lungful of air. The mountains around Silver City were riddled with spent mines. Zwing Hunt might as well have said they hid it somewhere in the Rockies. He poked his six-shooter a bit farther into the cell and cocked it. The sound of the hammer going back was louder than breaking bones.

"Where? Give me directions."

Slocum had waited too long. Hunt had regained what little courage he had. He sat straighter in the cell, more defiant. He shook his head and finally said, "Go on and kill me, Slocum. You'll never get the silver then."

"Satisfaction might be as good."

"Bullshit," Hunt said. "Think of it, Slocum. Tons of silver. That's what we got. I know where it is. If you want any of it, you need me."

"Just a kneecap. Maybe both of them. That's painful, I've heard tell. Or a shot to the gut. Might take you a week to die."

"You're bluffing. You didn't come here to kill me, and if you mess me up too much, I'll *never* talk. Look, Slocum, there's enough for both of us."

"Curly Bill and Sandy King might have beaten us to it. They got away." Slocum was thinking hard. Scaring the hiding place out of Hunt wasn't going to work. Slocum didn't like the deal the outlaw was likely to offer, but he didn't see any way around it.

"We turned the burros loose. There's no way they could get all the silver out of the mine shaft, even if they wanted it for themselves. There's got to be enough to make us filthy rich, Slocum. Both of us. All of us, if the Mexican bitch is still with you."

"She wants your hide for killing El Jéfe," Slocum said, almost revealing that the bandido was Belicia's brother. "And you stole her statue."

"That wood statue with all the gold and jewels? Curly Bill took a real shine to it." Zwing Hunt hesitated. Slocum saw the slow, sly grin cross the outlaw's face like a cloud scudding away from the sun. "It's with the silver. Break me out and I'll show you where we hid the silver—and the statue."

Slocum released the hammer and let it down gently on the loaded cylinder. As much as he wanted to end this miserable snake's life, he needed him.

"Slocum, wait!" Hunt's moment of apprehension that Slocum was going to leave him showed the man's fear. He had played his hand well until that moment. Now Slocum knew he had a hold over him.

"I'll see you in the Yuma Penitentiary if you cross me," Slocum snarled. That was a worse threat for Zwing Hunt than offering to ventilate him and leave his carcass for the buzzards.

"Get me out of here and we'll all be rich. Leave me and you'll never see so much as a glimmer of the silver."

"It won't take a minute," Slocum said. There wasn't time for elaborate planning, watching the sheriff's schedule, getting the deputy drunk—any of the things that meant a clean jailbreak. Slocum walked around and waved to Belicia. The woman hurried over.

"The statue," she whispered. "Does he know where it is?"

"We're breaking him out now. Get your horse saddled. That old nag might not gallop but it's better than nothing. And see about Hunt's horse."

"It's in the stable down the street," Belicia said. "I saw it when we bought my horse." She stared dubiously at her swaybacked nag. "We should get another if we are to run."

"No time," Slocum said, thinking hard. Breaking Hunt out was one thing, stealing a horse was another. They all might swing for the latter if the sheriff caught them. On the other hand, the sheriff might not even bother to chase them if Hunt broke out. Hughes had swung and Doc Neal was dead. The sheriff might think this was a fitting end to the Hughes Bunch.

"I will get his horse and be back in five minutes." Belicia looked at Slocum for a moment and then added, "Be careful." She gave him a quick kiss and rushed off to get Hunt's horse.

Slocum watched her go, wondering if she felt anything for him or only saw his cooperation as a means to recovering her precious santo. He couldn't tell, and that weighed down on him. Slocum shrugged it off and walked past the front of the jail. The deputy snored loudly inside, still asleep at his desk. The fight at the saloon had quieted and the sheriff hadn't returned with anyone for the lockup. If there was any luck left in the world, the sheriff and the bar brawlers were sharing a drink.

Slocum waited until he saw Belicia riding toward the jail with Hunt's and his own chestnut in tow. Slocum drew his Colt and walked into the office. The deputy stirred, still more asleep than awake. A quick blow to the side of the head put the deputy back down, never knowing what hit him. Slocum fumbled in the desk drawer, found the keys, and unlocked the outer door. He stalked to the rear of the jailhouse and saw Zwing Hunt waiting for him.

The outlaw's expression was a mixture of fear and anticipation of freedom. He bolted from the cell when Slocum unlocked it.

"You won't regret this, Slocum," he said. "I know where the silver is hidden. It's a place Hughes used a couple times before."

"Tell me now," Slocum said, pulling his six-shooter and aiming it at Hunt's face.

"John, he comes!" came Belicia's cry from outside. Slocum cursed under his breath. He knew who she meant. The sheriff had chosen the worst time possible to feel virtuous about being on duty.

"Get moving. We'll settle this when we're out of town," Slocum said, motioning for Hunt to precede him.

It was good that Slocum made Zwing Hunt go in front of him. Hunt walked into a bullet the instant he stepped out of the cell block. Slocum shot past the man's ear and sent the sheriff scrambling for cover. There wasn't time to do more than catch Hunt under his arms and support him as they got to the door.

The sheriff shot several more times but Belicia had positioned the horses to protect Slocum and Hunt.

"Help him," Slocum called to Belicia. He grunted as he hoisted Hunt's belly down over his saddle. The man stirred and tried to help, but he was losing strength fast. The sheriff's bullet had been much too accurate.

Slocum vaulted into the saddle, ducked as the sheriff fired a sixth time, and then cursed as he started reloading. Slocum knew they had a few minutes grace before the lawman opened up on them again. He put his spurs deep into the chestnut's flanks and got her running. Belicia and Hunt rode side by side as they followed him out of Silver City.

"What are we going to do?" asked Belicia. "My horse is already tiring and we haven't gone far."

Slocum looked around and saw they were less than a quarter mile away from the lockup. The sheriff wasn't the kind of man to let a jailbreak go unnoticed, and the deputy would insist on getting the escaped prisoner back since he had been made to look like a fool. He might not tell the sheriff he'd been sleeping on duty, but the evidence was clear that he had allowed a prisoner to escape.

Two lawmen came after them. And the cavalry. And the Apaches. And they still didn't know where Jim Hughes had hidden the silver.

Slocum hit the ground running and swung around to grab the reins on Hunt's horse. He slid the man off the saddle. For a second Slocum thought Hunt had died on him. Then eyelids flickered and he looked up. Dried lips formed a word that Slocum didn't understand.

"Where's the silver?" he demanded.

"The statue. Ask him of the blessed Virgin Mary," Belicia insisted.

Slocum held Zwing Hunt in his arms and knew the man wasn't going to answer much of anything he didn't want. He was so pale there had to be a lot of bleeding going on inside. The sheriff's bullet had torn through his chest and ripped up a lung. Pink froth appeared on Hunt's lips, a sure sign he was drowning in his own blood.

"Thanks, Slocum. You tried."

"Where—" Slocum didn't get much further with his questioning. Zwing Hunt coughed a gob of bloody phlegm. Face as pale as death, the man stared up at Slocum, but he didn't really see him.

"The Virgin Mary," pleaded Belicia. "Where is it?" She dropped to her knees and shook Hunt until his eyelids moved again. If force of will could make a man return to life, Belicia was giving Zwing Hunt more than enough. "Where is it?" she repeated.

"Curly Bill's in Tombstone," Hunt said. Then he died.

"We've got to find him before he tangles with Earp," said Slocum. "That's the only reason Bill would go into Arizona Territory. There're a dozen warrants out for his arrest."

Belicia looked up and turned her head. "I hear horses. A posse?"

"Take Hunt's horse," Slocum ordered. "It's stronger. And let's not waste any more time here." He didn't even look back where Zwing Hunt lay face up in the road. The man was dead, and that was about all Slocum could have wanted from him. His only regret was Hunt not giving them more information.

It took a week of dodging to get free of the Silver City sheriff and his determined posse. By then Slocum was almost willing to give up on tracking down Curly Bill. Almost. The lure of tons of silver kept him going, just as retrieving her santo kept Belicia in the saddle.

"There it is," Slocum said, hooking a leg around his saddle pommel and leaning forward slightly to ease the pain in his hindquarters. They had almost lived in the saddle this past week and it had filled him with more aches and pains than he wanted to count.

"It is so . . . nothing," Belicia finished weakly. She weaved as she rode, fatigue taking its toll on her, also. But Slocum had to agree. Tombstone wasn't much of a town. It had gone through boom and bust and new booms. Now it was hardly more than a pile of ramshackle buildings down the road from the cemetery.

"I want to find Curly Bill before nightfall," Slocum said. He squinted into the bright disk of the setting sun. This deadline gave him less than an hour before whatever life there was in the sleepy town stirred and came out of its daytime burrow. Swinging his leg back and getting his foot secure in the stirrup, he flicked the reins and got his trusty chestnut mare moving down the dusty road. He had eaten enough dirt in the past month for a lifetime. He vowed to never again ride horseback when he got the silver.

He could buy his own rail car like Leland Stanford. Hell, he could buy an entire railroad and travel wherever the mood sent him. And there would always be a full bottle of whiskey, the finest Kentucky bourbon he could buy, not the cheap trade whiskey he was usually served. And women. He wanted women, lovely ones, willing ones who would give him what he'd never had before.

The thought made him turn and look out of the corner of his eye at Belicia. She rode with a grim determination. What role did she play in his life after he got his share of the silver? She claimed she wanted nothing more than the santo. Would she deliver the relic to her village's church and ride away with him or did the future hold something different for her?

Slocum wished he knew. But he realized he was putting the cart before the horse. He couldn't buy fine clothing and whiskey and entire railroads until he got the silver Hughes had hidden. To do that, he had to find out from Curly Bill or Sandy King where it was buried.

"How will we locate him?" Belicia asked.

Slocum almost laughed. "Finding him'll be the easy part. Making Bill tell us where the silver and the statue are will be a damn sight harder." She knew Curly Bill's temperament as well as he did. The man was a stone killer, without mercy. Worse than this, Curly Bill enjoyed the bloodshed. He had been too young to fight in the war, but he would have appreciated the slaughter.

In spite of the heat, Slocum shivered. Curly Bill would have been bosom buddies with Quantrill and Bloody Bill Anderson.

They rode down the main street, looking at both sides for some sign of the man they sought. Slocum noticed how Belicia moved ever closer when she realized there weren't any buildings save for saloons and dancehalls here. The evening's rowdy festivities were starting already with hard rock gold miners coming into town to spend their meager wages on cheap whiskey and willing women. A few shots rang out, but no one took notice of it. There might even be a killing or two before the law would come to investigate. Tombstone was a wide-open town, for all its poverty and boom-bust economy.

"Look there," Belicia said. Slocum felt frost forming in the air, quickly replaced by hot fury. He had to reach out and grab her arm, almost pulling her out of the saddle.

"Don't," he cautioned. "Let me handle this."

"It's José's saddle. He stole my brother's saddle!"

Slocum had seen the flashy silver chasing on the saddle an instant after Belicia. There was no doubt either Curly Bill or Sandy King was here. Robbing a dead man looked to be Curly Bill's style.

"If you fail, I will torture him. I have heard how the Yaquis put a man's feet to the fire and burn him by inches. They flay the skin from his bones and crush his testicles. It takes days to die. Curly Bill will die this way!"

"You miserable son of a bitch!" came the angry cry. "You're nothing but a lily-livered snake. Go on, turn tail and run. Let me see your backside!"

Slocum recognized Curly Bill's voice coming from inside the Prickly Pear Saloon. He dismounted, slipped the leather thong off the hammer of his Colt Navy, and prepared to face the man. He turned just as the man exploded from the saloon.

"Out here, you horse's ass. You get your cowardly bones out here right now!"

"Bill!" Slocum called. "I want to—" Slocum never got any farther. A rugged looking man with a battered tin star pinned on his coat's lapel followed Curly Bill from the saloon. Slocum had never seen Wyatt Earp before, but the handlebar mustache, the fancy duds, and the wintry look in his eye branded this man as something out of the ordinary, even for Tombstone.

"Stop them, John. You must!" Belicia started to run to Bill. Slocum held her back. There was no way in hell he was going to get between Curly Bill and Marshal Earp.

"Draw or not, whatever pleases you," said Earp.

Slocum might have seen a man draw faster, but he couldn't remember when. Earp fired a second shot before Curly Bill's hand even closed on the handle of his six-shooter. Bill stared down stupidly at the two holes in his chest, slowly turning red and spreading. He looked up, as if he was going to say something, then simply collapsed like a marionette with its strings cut.

Slocum watched Wyatt Earp stride forward, roll Curly Bill over with the toe of his boot, then stick his .44 back into his holster. He turned and walked off. The marshal had just killed Slocum's only chance to recover the Monterrey silver.

17

"I won't give up." Belicia sat with her back against the board wall of the stable where they'd spent the night, arms crossed on her chest and her legs drawn up tightly. The set to her mouth told Slocum she wasn't talking just to hear her own voice. She meant it.

"Curly Bill's not going to tell us. Neither are Hughes, Doc Neal, or Hunt. That leaves Sandy King, but we don't know what happened to him after he hightailed it out of Silver City."

"We can find him. If you won't go with me, *I* shall find him," Belicia said with icy determination. "You should never have let this Earp person kill Curly Bill. He was our road to the statue."

"To the silver," Slocum said, getting mad at Belicia's implication of cowardice. He wasn't going to walk between a mad-dog killer like Curly Bill and a man with Wyatt Earp's reputation. Earp had been fast, damned fast. Slocum wasn't sure he could beat him in a fair fight. Hell, he wasn't sure he could beat him in any kind of fight. The men who thought

146

they were the fastest guns were the ones next to Curly Bill out in the town cemetery.

Curly Bill hadn't even merited having a boot taken off and used as his headstone. Before the town undertaker had gotten the body out to Boot Hill, someone had stolen Bill's boots and pistol. Tombstone was that kind of community.

"Who cares about the silver? People's souls are at stake, and you let Earp kill him."

"I didn't let the marshal do anything," Slocum snapped angrily. "He's fast, and he's the law around here. Curly Bill had always thought he could take Earp, and now we know he wasn't up to it. But none of that's my fault. I wanted him as bad as you. Our reasons might be different, but I wanted Curly Bill."

"I am sorry, John," she said, but her tone still carried the bite of fury he had felt before. "The Virgin Mary is important. I still get angry when I think of how Bill shot splinters from it. No one should do that. May he burn in hell forever."

Slocum knew Curly Bill was likely to do just that. He couldn't remember a kind word or deed the man had ever done. And nobody liked him. Slocum had made a point of never turning his back on him. But none of that mattered. Bill was dead and buried and they had to find Sandy King if they wanted to get what each of them treasured most.

"I'll ask around. Maybe King came to Tombstone with Curly Bill. If so, he'll be trying to make tracks to keep Earp from taking him on, too. I might be able to find the dust cloud."

"Do what you will," Belicia said. "I will see to the horses."

"We're running low on money," Slocum pointed out. "Don't get too fancy with them."

"I know how to tend animals. My life has not been one of complete sheltering." She stared at him with her hot eyes, and he felt like melting. Belicia Salazar was pretty when she smiled. When she was angry she was gorgeous.

"Didn't mean anything by it," Slocum said. "I'll be back soon."

Belicia graced him with a tiny smile. He turned and left, heading for a saloon. He knew how she felt. They had missed getting to Curly Bill by minutes. If Earp hadn't come along when he had, they might have been able to torture the information from Bill. After all the Hughes Bunch had done to him and Belicia, Slocum wasn't above using a few of the Yaqui tortures Belicia had mentioned. And he knew a few Apache methods of making life miserable. Some of them he had learned firsthand.

Curly Bill was gone, and they had to find Sandy King. Slocum went into the Prickly Pear Saloon since this was the last place Bill had been. Though it was hardly nine in the morning, the place buzzed about how fast Earp had cut down Curly Bill and how the Clantons were damned fools for wanting to take on Earp and his brothers. The talk settled down and eventually turned to who was prospecting and what they were finding—all bald-faced lies, if Slocum was any judge.

He stood at one end of the long bar, nursing a single shot of trade whiskey. He could have put the gunpowder in the whiskey to better use in his Colt Navy, but he didn't complain. The others in the saloon eagerly poured and drank the same concoction. Eventually the barkeep came over and leaned against the wall, studying the room.

"You just drifting through Tombstone?" he asked Slocum.

"Looking for a friend," Slocum said. "Reckon I'd better not mention his name, though, not after what happened when I rode in last night around dusk."

"You knew Curly Bill?"

"Didn't like the son of a bitch, if that's what you mean," Slocum said. "He was a braggart and a blowhard. Earp gave him what for."

"Deserved it," the barkeep agreed. "Want another?" He stared at the almost untouched shot of whiskey. Slocum knew what the man was asking and fished in his pocket until he found his last silver Mexican coin. He dropped it on the bar. Its ring was music to his ears.

And he'd never hear its equal for a long, long time if the barkeep wasn't able to put him onto Sandy King's trail.

"He was a friend of Curly Bill's," Slocum said. "Name of King."

The barkeep shook his head slowly. Slocum shifted slightly, ready to grab for the coin if the bartender tried to pocket it without giving him anything useful. Finally the barkeep smiled and nodded, the memory returning.

"Curly Bill said he and a friend had just rode in from Silver City. Think this is the fella you're looking for?"

"Could be," Slocum allowed. "Where might I find him?"

"He rode in with Bill, that much I remember. Might have stayed but he never came in here if he did. More'n likely, he saw that Curly Bill was going to tangle with Earp and just blowed on out."

"Where to?"

"Yes sir, never saw a man so intent on getting himself killed. You got to see Earp in a fight to appreciate how quick that man is. Greased lightning ain't half as fast. I heard tell he grabbed a jackrabbit by the throat as it leaped out of its burrow. Fast, damned fast."

Slocum couldn't have cared less about the tall tales surrounding Wyatt Earp. He sipped at the whiskey and tried not to make a face. It twisted and turned down his throat like a rusty corkscrew and exploded in his belly with the force of four sticks of rotted dynamite.

"Good, ain't it?"

The barkeep didn't make any move to give Slocum another, and Slocum wasn't going to pass over the silver coin unless he got something more about Sandy King.

"If King did come into Tombstone with Bill, where might he have gone?"

"I'm beginning to remember now. Bill said something about his friend's horse dyin' under him. Hard road from Silver City. The desert's no place for a weak animal. Must have gone back toward New Mexico. There was a stage what left last Tuesday."

That was well nigh a week back. Slocum tried to keep down his rising gorge. The liquor burned and cut at his innards, but it was excitement more than anything else bringing back up the contents of his belly.

"Where'd the stagecoach head?"

"Ask over at the office. Tell the little lady working there that Jackson sent you. That'll warm her up to you."

"Thanks," Slocum said, making no move to take back the ten peso coin. He heard a faint scrapping noise as he turned to go and knew the money had vanished instantly, Jackson putting it into his vest pocket as he took the empty glass.

Slocum had less than ten dollars left, five of it in greenbacks that were damned near worthless in a town like Tombstone where hard coin meant everything. He doubted if Belicia had that much. But he had a hint of King's destination. All he needed was to ask at the stagecoach office. He paused outside the office, wondering if it was a smart thing for him to go in and tell the woman working there that the barkeep had sent him.

He kept walking and went back to the stable. Belicia had finished feeding the animals and was working on two others stabled there. The owner sat in the tack room, swilling cheap whiskey from a bottle. Slocum frowned.

"He will let us stay for nothing if I curry the other horses," she said simply.

"I might know how to find where Sandy King went," Slocum said, pulling her away. The stable owner scowled darkly but didn't come out to argue with a man like Slocum. "I need you to do the asking, though."

"Why is this?"

"Just a feeling I've got. The clerk over at the stagecoach office is the one we have to get the information from, and

I was told that she was sweet on the saloon keeper, name of Jackson."

Belicia smiled. "You are not so sure of this. You think if this Jackson is mentioned, the clerk will say nothing more?"

"Might be a scam they've got going, maybe not. She might want to spit on the ground where he's walked, and he doesn't believe it. If a woman asks another woman, there's no hard feelings."

Belicia laughed at this. "You know nothing of women if you think this, but I will ask. King took the stage out of town?"

"Maybe last Tuesday, heading back into New Mexico. That's all I could find out." Slocum wiped the sweat from his forehead. It wasn't even noon and already the heat was oppressive.

"You are pale. Are you feeling well, John?"

"Not too good, now that you mention it. Might have been the whiskey the barkeep sold me. Tore at my gut like a wildcat."

"I will find out what I can. Lie down and try to rest. You look like death itself." She took his hand and led him toward a stall. The stable owner perked up at the sight. Slocum heard the man coming out of the tack room, trying to walk quietly. He might as well have been walking through a room filled with long-tailed cats for all the good it did him. Slocum knew what the owner thought was going to happen, and what he was going to watch.

He found himself staring down the barrel of Slocum's Colt.

"Sorry," Slocum said insincerely. "Thought you were someone trying to spy on us."

"Just coming to see how the little lady's doin' with the horses. You can stay another night if you feed and curry them again." His pudgy face beaded with sweat when Slocum didn't put the six-shooter away. "Anything you two wantin'? I was on my way over to Ned Peterson's store."

"That is kind of you. We need nothing," Belicia said, keeping from laughing. Only when the man vanished like a heat mirage did Slocum put his pistol away.

"Snoop. Hate them all," Slocum said. He wobbled a mite, then sat down. This wasn't like him. The stable spun in crazy circles, and his legs had turned watery.

"I will be back soon. There is only the one clerk?"

"Reckon so. That's all Jackson told me about. He might just have eyes for the one." Slocum laid on the fragrant hay and in seconds drifted off to a deep sleep. The next thing he knew, Belicia dropped down beside him. He came awake with a start, hand reaching for his Colt, disoriented and trying to figure out why.

"It is all right, John. Everything is fine," soothed Belicia. "You have slept well all day."

"All day!" He sat bolt upright, still fighting down the dizziness. The sun had set and Tombstone was coming alive once more with the sound of distant music, laughter and occasional gunfire.

"I could not speak directly to the stagecoach office clerk," Belicia said. "The office manager did not like my looks."

"What? Why not?"

"He didn't want any Mexicans scaring away customers, he said. I waited until the clerk—her name is Martha and she *hates* Jackson—was permitted lunch."

"So you talked to her then, and she didn't have the prejudice against Mexicans that her boss did. So?" Slocum's head threatened to split like a rotten melon. He wondered if the liquor had poisoned him. Whatever Jackson put into his trade whiskey carried the kick of an epileptic mule.

"You rush on so," Belicia chided. "This is exciting. I have found what has happened to Sandy King."

"He's still in Tombstone?"

"No, no, he has gone on into New Mexico, as you thought."

"Where? He's got almost a week's head start on us. We ought to—" He tried standing but found that his legs weren't strong enough. He sank back to the pile of hay. Belicia lay beside him, her arm across his chest to keep him from trying to sit up again.

"You have no desire to find the statue of the Virgin Mary, do you?" she asked in a soft voice.

"The silver's all I want," Slocum said, fighting the throb building behind his eyes. "Where's King? There can't be too many places a stagecoach from Tombstone could go into New Mexico."

"Shakespeare," she muttered.

"What?" Slocum turned to her and stared into her eyes. He wasn't sure what he read there. Passion, maybe. Fire, definitely. But he didn't know if it was directed his way or at the quest for the santo until she kissed him full on the lips. Then there could be no mistaking her desire. Her hands roamed up and down the front of his body, poking and prodding, stroking and squeezing until he began to respond.

"Can't do this," he said. "Too dizzy. World's all turned around."

"It is nice to know I affect you so," she said, her tongue working its way wetly into his ear. Slocum collapsed back into the hay, not wanting to fight her. He felt himself responding more and more as her fingers began squeezing rhythmically. He moaned softly as she opened his trousers and pulled out the steel-hard shaft she found there.

"That's not the least bit dizzy," he said, his head buzzing. He gasped when he felt her warm lips circling him, sucking hard, threatening to pull his seed from its hidden recesses. Her fingers tapped on the tight fleshy bag containing his balls, stroked and squeezed and made him feel as if he would explode at any instant.

Just when he knew he couldn't control himself any longer, her mouth vanished from his engorged tip. Cool air gusted in through the stable's open door and chilled him.

"What're you doing? Where are you going?"

Belicia hiked her skirts and straddled his waist. "We celebrate this night," she said. "You do not like this?"

She lowered herself over his groin. He felt her soft nether lips part and then he plunged deep into her as the woman simply relaxed. She twisted back and forth gently, stimulating him even more. He tried to roll her over, to get on top. His dizziness prevented it.

"Enjoy what I offer," Belicia said in her sultry voice. "I am enjoying this. So should you, John."

"I am, I do," he got out. He closed his eyes and let the sensations wash through his body. He opened his eyes and saw the expression of sheer desire on her face. He reached up and opened the buttons on her white blouse. Warm breasts tumbled out into his hands. He returned the favor she had bestowed earlier, kneading and squeezing, teasing and tormenting gently until the nipples stood out in bold relief.

She began rising and falling on his manhood, doing all the work. He experienced a flash of giddiness that passed. He wasn't going to be able to contribute more than he was already, and that suited both of them fine. Slocum let the woman work up and down, moving slowly at first and then picking up the pace until she gasped and sobbed constantly.

"So good, John, so very good," Belicia gasped out. "I need this. We are so close, so close!"

He didn't know if she was talking about them or being near to finding the silver. The santo. Sandy King. Everything. He lost his ability to think straight as Belicia began rising and falling around him faster and faster. Friction burned at his length. Pressure mounted once more inside, and this time he couldn't restrain himself. He clutched hard at the bucking woman's breasts.

Belicia tossed her head back, her long, dark hair flying like a banner as she let out a long, low shriek of pure ecstasy. Slocum felt her flesh tighten around his hidden length. This new compression on his sensitive member released the flood mounting inside him. He arched his back and lifted Belicia off her knees. She hung suspended on his body for a moment before he collapsed back.

Then they began grinding their crotches together, pushing each other's desire to the limit.

All too soon, Slocum sank back, spent. Belicia stretched out beside him, her hand resting on his shoulder and her naked breasts pressed against his side.

"We are good together, John," she said.

"King," he muttered, the haze closing in on his mind once more. He was dizzy and felt a little sick to his stomach and the lovemaking had tired him unduly.

"Yes, John, for the King we will do this, *and* his mother."

Slocum wasn't sure what she meant. He fell asleep almost instantly, lost in his dreams of silver.

18

Slocum awoke, feeling like he had the granddaddy of all hangovers. He struggled to sit up and held his head. The only positive reaction to this was the lack of dizziness. His headache had magnified, and he knew he was going to lose the contents of his belly, but the dizziness had passed. Then he looked around the stable and saw something else had gone.

"Belicia!"

Slocum struggled to his feet. Holding his head and keeping his gorge down, he saw that her horse was gone. He quickly saddled his chestnut mare, who balked at being ridden again. The animal had rested for almost two days. That ought to be enough for any saddle horse, Slocum decided. He swung into the saddle and started from the stable when the portly owner hailed him.

"Where you headin'?" Something in the way the man spoke alerted Slocum to danger.

"After my lady friend," he said. "You wouldn't happen to know when she left, would you?"

The leer on the stable owner's face convinced Slocum something was astir in Tombstone. And he would definitely not like it.

"Left before sunup, she did." The pudgy man looked expectant, as if a carnival parade would come down Tombstone's main street at any moment.

Slocum didn't bother asking further questions. The man seemed intent on keeping him here, and that meant Slocum had to get out of town in a hurry. He urged his mare forward. The man tried to grab his leg but Slocum kicked out and sent him reeling backward. Outside the stable, Slocum saw a small crowd gathered at the far end of the street. He went the other way.

He rode past the Prickly Pear Saloon, where the barkeep stood outside, squinting into the sun. Jackson hailed him. Slocum decided it was worth a few seconds to see if the bartender knew what the commotion was.

"Top of the morning to you," Jackson called. "You ever look up sweet li'l ole Martha over at the stagecoach office?"

"Can't say that I did. Decided it wasn't worth my effort," Slocum lied.

"She's a spirited gal, Martha is. She's real sweet on me." Slocum remembered what Belicia had told him and merely nodded. Jackson looked past Slocum to the end of the street. "You thinkin' on tangling with him?"

This caught Slocum off guard. He didn't know what the barkeep was talking about, but the coldness that formed in his gut told him it wasn't going to be his morning. Belicia's leaving was one thing; he could track her. But this was more serious.

"What do you mean?"

"Thought you'd be the one to know," Jackson said, frowning. "Seems Wyatt Earp's got it into his head that you and Curly Bill were partners. He wants to ask you about an army payroll robbery a month or so back."

"What did you tell Earp?"

"Me?" Jackson asked with mock surprise. "I don't know nothing about nothing, mister. I just tend bar. The Prickly Pear's a good saloon and I'd never—"

Slocum didn't waste time listening to what else Jackson wouldn't do. If Earp came in and demanded to know something, the barkeep would be the first to tell him. On his best day, Slocum might be able to match the marshal's blinding speed.

Maybe.

This was far from his best day. His hand wasn't shaking much any more and his vision had cleared. He didn't know if he'd picked up a touch of the ague or if the Prickly Pear's whiskey had poisoned him. Whatever the cause, he wasn't about to stand out in the middle of the street and answer questions put to him by Marshal Earp. More than likely, the questions would be punctuated with bullets. Slocum wasn't going to be a clay pigeon for Earp or any lawman.

"Hey, come on back," called Jackson. "I'll stand you to a free drink. On the house!"

Slocum kicked at his horse until it broke into a trot. He didn't want to tire the horse unduly. He might be in for a long ride if Earp took it into his head to form a posse—or just saddle up by himself—and come after Slocum.

Once he was a mile or so out of town, Slocum slowed to a walk and began getting his bearings. The sun was just poking up over the distant mountains, his destination. Belicia wouldn't head back to Silver City. There was no hope of finding Sandy King there. But she had found out where King had gone on the stage.

Shakespeare. Slocum didn't know exactly where in New Mexico Territory it was, but it was south of Silver City and still in the vicinity where the Hughes Bunch had hidden the silver. All he had to do was ride for New Mexico, and he would cross Belicia's trail.

He found her just after sundown. Her small campfire hadn't been banked properly and he saw both the smoke and the fire itself. He dismounted, tethered his tired horse and approached the camp on foot. He made sure he'd taken the leather thong off the hammer of his Colt Navy before getting too close. A nasty thought had worn at him all day, like a burr under a saddle blanket.

"Good evening, Belicia," he said. She jumped, reaching for the rifle still in its saddle sheath. When she saw who had spoken, she relaxed. But Slocum didn't.

"You startled me, John. I didn't expect to see you again."

"Didn't think I'd come after you?"

"I doubted that you remembered the name of the town where King was headed," she said. "You showed no desire to help me recover the santo. I decided it was best if I did it on my own."

"You didn't have to tell the marshal I'd been mixed up with the Hughes Bunch and the cavalry payroll robbery." He watched as her dark eyes widened and caught light from the fire.

"I never did this thing. You believe I would—"

"You talk about the statue of the Virgin Mary, but three tons of silver would buy that village of yours a heap more than a relic to pray to."

"All I want is the Virgin Mary," she said firmly, and he almost believed her.

"You shouldn't have left me like that. It makes me suspicious."

"I am sorry if your faith is so weak," Belicia said, settling back down, well away from her rifle. Slocum remained cautious.

"Seems it was *your* faith in me that was weak," he said. "I told you I'd help find the statue."

"What are you going to do now?"

Slocum didn't have a good answer for that. If he took all the silver, it was still more than he could spend in a lifetime. Half of it might be more than he'd ever be able to spend, but the notion of a railroad car all to himself, whiskey, and women seemed more appealing. And Belicia wasn't part of that dream.

"We can go on together," she said. "There is no reason to trust each other. I want the statue, you want the silver. We can both get what we want."

"There's no way I could spend all the silver by myself," Slocum said, watching her reaction closely. "You deserve some of it. Maybe half, if we're the only two left."

"Sandy King is left."

Slocum didn't answer the unstated question left hanging in the air. King wouldn't be needing his share when Slocum finished with him. King as much as Curly Bill and the others had double-crossed him. Nobody did that and got away with it. He was undecided about the lengths of Belicia's perfidy and what he should do about it. Ever since their first meeting, she had been veiled in secrecy, leaving him to walk on emotional quicksand with her.

"We can ride together," he decided. "When we find King, we'll see what has to be done."

"This is good," she said. Belicia stretched like a cat, then lay back as if expecting Slocum to lie beside her. He shook his head. She looked disappointed, but Slocum wasn't sure where the core of her dissatisfaction lay. To sleep with her again was folly. It might even be suicidal.

Slocum couldn't know for sure but Belicia might have poisoned him back in Tombstone so she could ride on to Shakespeare and find Sandy King, get the silver and just vanish into the middle of Mexico again. He doubted it, but Belicia was a clever woman and one who had kept him guessing a long time.

Sleeping without a blanket kept him alert but left him groggy in the morning. And riding while sleeping was almost impossible over the rugged terrain, but Slocum managed somehow. They reached Shakespeare three days later.

"Not much to it. Wonder why King decided to come here?" Slocum asked aloud. He didn't expect Belicia to answer.

They hadn't spoken more than a dozen words in the past three hours, and that suited him just fine. The distance between them had grown larger than the Barranca del Cobre and was probably harder to bridge now.

"It must be close to the where the santo is hidden," she said.

"The silver," he corrected. Slocum cursed himself for baiting her like this. He turned his attention to the small New Mexico town. It was hardly more than a main street and a pair of cross streets, but it had a vitality to it lacking even in Tombstone. The people here weren't totally dependent on mining. There must be ranches in the area—people producing cattle and crops—in addition to the obvious mining activity throughout the region.

They rode slowly into the town and down the main street, Avon Avenue. Whoever had founded the town had been an avid fan of Shakespeare. Everything carried some reference to the limey, or so Slocum guessed. There were two hotels, a general store that was stocked with anything a rancher or miner might need, and a saloon that rivaled those Slocum had seen in San Francisco. Slocum walked under the gilt-edged sign hanging over the doorway of the saloon. Once past the etched glass panels in the door, he saw red velvet hangings, a discreet painted nude behind the long polished bar, and gaming tables covered with green felt. It was a place Slocum wouldn't mind spending time in.

"John, everyone is watching us." Belicia shivered as if taken by a chill.

He saw that she was right. The entire town couldn't number more than two hundred, and they had all gathered to watch him and Belicia ride down Avon Avenue. Slocum knew why they might want to stare at Belicia; she was a gorgeous woman, even after such a long time on the trail. But their attention made his uneasiness grow.

The town sheriff moseyed out and leaned against the hitching post in front of the jail, thumbs thrust into his gunbelt. He spat into the street, took a moment to get a plug of new chew, then returned his steely-eyed observation of the newcomers.

"We can't just ride on out," Slocum said to Belicia. "It's time to take the bull by the horns." He smiled at the people gathered, tipped his hat to one or two of the ladies who chastely averted their eyes then chanced a quick look at him after he rode past. Slocum reined in and dismounted, using the same hitching post where the sheriff was leaning.

"Morning, Sheriff," Slocum greeted. "We're looking for someone and you might just be the one who can help us."

The sheriff looked from Slocum to the worn ebony handle of his six-shooter and then to Belicia. His eyes lingered for a moment, then darted back to Slocum.

"Do I know you, mister?"

Slocum hoped that the sheriff wasn't the kind to study wanted posters. He had made the bold move because they were so obviously the center of attention that it wouldn't have done any good to try and hide. Better to brazen it out.

"Can't figure how," Slocum said. "The lady and I are visiting your fine town for the first time."

"Just visitin'? Not plannin' on stayin'?"

"Afraid not," Slocum said.

"We are looking for Sandy King," Belicia said. Slocum wished she had been more circumspect. Something was wrong in Shakespeare, and he wanted to find out what it was before trotting out the name of a man likely to be known as a criminal.

"Well now, ma'am, you've come to the right place. He's in the back room." The sheriff jerked his thumb over his shoulder, indicating the jailhouse. Slocum studied the rundown sheriff's office. It was the only building out of place in the entire town. Shakespeare was well kept and peaceable enough. The jailhouse looked ready to fall down if anybody so much as spit against a wall. Bullet holes marred the wood and a pane of glass had been broken some time back and never replaced.

"You've got him in the lockup?" Slocum asked. "Nothing serious, I hope."

"Well, he got to town well nigh a week ago and started making trouble," the sheriff said slowly, as if choosing his words. He watched both Slocum and Belicia for their reaction. Slocum adopted his best poker face and hoped Belicia would do the same. For all his hick appearance and drawl, the sheriff was a smart man. From the look of the heavy .45 thrust into his holster, he was also a dangerous one.

"That's King for you," Slocum said. "Shot up the saloon, I'd wager."

"That he did, that he did." The sheriff spat again. He didn't replace the tobacco. "He got drunk and shot the finger off a merchant, just as a joke, he said. Well, let me tell you, old Mr. Keller was not inclined to take losing his pinky finger as any joke."

"Reckon not," Slocum said.

"We don't hold with such behavior in Shakespeare. Used to be a lot of mining in these parts. I kept the town quiet in spite of unruly miners comin' in to blow off steam. Lonely life out in the hills. Nobody to talk to but the coyotes and rattlesnakes."

"So King is doing time for shooting a citizen of Shakespeare?" asked Belicia. "Can we talk with him?"

"Don't see why not," the sheriff said. He took his time pulling out a pocket watch and studying its face. "You'd better hurry, though. King's not going to be in the cell much past noon. That gives you about fifteen minutes."

Slocum was put on his guard by the way the sheriff spoke, but he didn't care about the details. If he could talk to Sandy King and convince him he was a dead man when he stepped out of the cell at noon, he might open up and tell Slocum where the Hughes Bunch had hidden the silver.

"We want to see him, Sheriff," Slocum said. "You need my pistol?"

"Rules are rules. Nobody gets back into the cellblock wearing a sidearm. Makes sense, if you think about it."

Slocum wasn't pleased to hand over his Colt, but he wanted to see King. Belicia crowded past him and squirted into the narrow corridor leading back to the twin cells. Slocum hung back for a moment to see if the sheriff was going to accompany them.

"I'll stay out here in the office till you're done. Remember what I said. You got fifteen minutes, no more." The sheriff sat on his desk, a sawed-off shotgun laying beside him. The lawman smiled crookedly and said, "Can't do a dang thing with this scattergun since I loaded it with carpet tacks to break up a riot over at the saloon. Guess I have to keep usin' it that way."

Slocum said nothing. The sheriff was letting him know that gunning down a dozen people, maybe cutting them in half just to stop a fight, wasn't out of the question for him. The town of Shakespeare was stranger than Slocum had thought when he first saw it.

"Tell me where the santo is, King," pleaded Belicia. Tears rolled down her cheeks and left salty tracks.

Slocum was slow going back to where Belicia pleaded with Sandy King. The woman wasn't the only one in the cellblock crying. A man in the other cell sat on the bunk, head in hands, and wept openly. Slocum stopped and stared at him. The man looked up, his face ugly with fear.

"Get me out, mister. I beg you!"

"What's wrong?" Slocum saw the man was almost unable to stop crying.

"I stole a horse and they're hangin' me!"

Slocum had heard of worse punishment for horse thieves. He dismissed the man from his thoughts and went back to talk with King. A man ought to be brave enough to take the consequences of his deeds.

"Tell me, please," begged Belicia, rattling the bars. Sandy King sat on his bunk, legs pulled up and his face pale. His hands shook. He scrambled to his feet when he saw Slocum.

"You got to get me out of here, Slocum. You've got to!"

"Where's the silver buried?" Slocum asked without pre-
amble. "Tell me where it is."

"And the statue of the blessed virgin," added Belicia.

"Get me out and I'll show you. You got to do it quick.
You're the only one who can do it. The silver for my
freedom, Slocum."

Slocum had heard the same dickering with Zwing Hunt,
and trying to break Hunt out of the Silver City had led to
his death. But the Silver City jail was far more difficult to
crack than this one. All Slocum had to do was tie a rope
around the bars in the jail cell window and pull. The entire
wall might come off.

"Why are you so anxious to get sprung? The sheriff said
he was letting you out at noon."

"God, Slocum, there's going to be a hanging."

"The horse thief in the next cell. He told me." Slocum's
eyes narrowed when he saw the expression on King's face.
He guessed what the man was going to say before he opened
his mouth to speak.

"And me. They're stringing me up, too, just for blowing
some old fool's little finger off!"

"You are lying," Belicia cried. "They do not hang people
for this. You are trying to keep from telling us where the
santo is hidden!"

"Tell her to shut up, Slocum. I'm serious. They're going
to hang me along with the horse thief. I ain't done nothing.
They can't do this to me."

"Did they even give you a trial?"

"They called it that. I was convicted before the trial
started. They're going to hang me for shootin' an old coot's
finger off—me, who robbed the Monterrey mint!" Sandy
King was growing hysterical. Slocum glanced at his brother's watch and saw the reason. It was five minutes until
twelve. Time crushed down on him like all three tons of
silver dropped from above.

"Tell us. We deserve the loot," Slocum said. He gripped
Belicia's arm to keep her quiet. Distracting King now less-

ened their chances of finding where the Hughes Bunch had hidden the silver.

"Get me out. Keep 'em from hanging me and you'll be rich. Hell, keep it all. I won't care if I'm alive. I can get more. Tons of it, Slocum. Think of it. And it'll all be yours if you—" Sandy King bit off the rest. The sheriff opened the door and came back, the sawed-off shotgun resting in the crook of his left arm. Behind him crowded a dozen men, all armed with rifles and six-guns.

"We're here for you boys," the sheriff said. "The judge said to swing you at noon. Reckon it'll take about five minutes to walk over to the stagecoach depot."

"Why there?" asked Slocum, intrigued in spite of himself.

The sheriff grinned like a wolf showing its fangs. "We decided to play a little trick on the folks arriving on the afternoon stage. We're gonna leave these owlhoots strung up. Can't wait to see the faces on those passengers when they walk in and see two men dangling from the rafters."

The men with the sheriff laughed uproariously at this practical joke. Several men cut off Slocum and Belicia, pressing them against the back wall. Sandy King kicked and shouted, but the three men pulling him from the cell had no problem. The crying horse thief went along peaceably enough, Slocum thought, but he was still crying and pleading not to be hanged.

"You two are welcome to come over for the festivities at noon," the sheriff said, his shotgun aimed in their direction. "Mrs. Ollens done made some of her truly fine potato salad, and Mrs. Bennet's fried up a batch of chicken just for the occasion."

"We . . . we'll be there, Sheriff," Slocum said. The lawman ushered them from the jail, returned Slocum's pistol to him, then hurried on to the stagecoach depot.

"They cannot do this," Belicia said, tears running freely down her cheeks. "He must tell us where the Virgin Mary is!"

Slocum looked beyond that to the party atmosphere in Shakespeare. Hangings were sometimes solemn events, depending on who was getting strung up and what crime was committed. But he had seldom seen such an outright festive air when it came to hanging a horse thief and a man guilty of nothing more than shooting off a gent's finger.

"What are we going to do?" Slocum asked, thinking out loud. He didn't expect Belicia to have an answer. He wasn't sure there was one. The only man still alive who knew where the silver had been hidden was going to take that secret with him to his grave—and Slocum had to save him.

"We get our rifles and ride up and rescue him," Belicia said. "We can do it. They are all preparing for the party. They will not expect it of us."

Slocum saw she was wrong on this score. The people of Shakespeare had been gathering for the hanging, but they were still curious about the two strangers who had ridden into town just minutes before the necktie party. Dozens of men watched closely. Even more studied Belicia with a mixture of curiosity and lust. The women who lined the street were spending more and more time watching Belicia, also. Hate or envy—he couldn't be sure what the overriding emotion was. But the women of Shakespeare weren't going to just up and ignore Belicia right now.

"I don't know how we're going to save him," Slocum said, feeling trapped. He started worrying that Sandy King might make a last minute confession implicating Slocum in the army payroll robbery and the mint robbery and anything else that might keep him from swinging. If he tried, there wasn't enough time for Slocum and Belicia to make a run for it.

A town this hungry to stretch a criminal's neck might just decide to hang two more and make it a day-long feast.

"You know him, don't you?" asked a man from the boardwalk in front of the hotel. "Why not ask the sheriff to give you a front row seat? We can afford to be hospitable here in Shakespeare. We're good people."

Slocum smiled crookedly and pushed Belicia toward the stagecoach depot. There might be something they could do. Some small thing that would allow them to save King and find out where the silver was.

"You came over to see your friend depart this world?" asked the sheriff. "Reckon I misjudged you. Didn't think you had the stomach for it. Chester, you see that these two get good seats so they won't miss anything."

Slocum was aware of the sheriff's shotgun moving restlessly like a coiled snake's head seeking a target. If he made a move for his six-shooter, the sheriff would blow off his head.

"John, no," Belicia said in a small voice. She stared at the center of the room. Both prisoners had their hands tied behind them and had been put on chairs. Men drew lots to see who got to put the nooses around their necks. Slocum hoped the lottery might go on long enough to give him time to free King, but it was over too quick.

"Slocum, you've got to do something," King pleaded. "I know where it is. I'll tell you."

"Get on with it, will you? The potato salad's waiting for us!" the sheriff called from behind Slocum.

Before Slocum could even blink, two men had grabbed Sandy King's chair and yanked it from under him. He fell less than two feet but it was enough to snap his neck.

The horse thief went seconds later with the same result.

Slocum hurried to the dangling outlaw's side, thinking he might lift him if he was choking. The fall had broken his neck, but it hadn't killed him outright.

"Where, King, where is it?" Slocum demanded.

"Sk—" was all he choked out before he died.

"Step on back now, gents. Let Digger O'Dell through. He's got a spot picked out for these two varmints, but he needs to measure them first." The sheriff herded Slocum and Belicia away from the slowly twisting bodies as the undertaker measured them for cheap coffins. At least the people of Shakespeare were civilized enough to give them a decent burial.

"Come on out and let's eat. The stagecoach won't be in for a couple hours yet," the sheriff said. What he'd said about leaving the bodies to scare the stage's passengers looked to be the truth. The crowd hurried out to partake of the fried chicken and potato salad, and the barkeep rolled a keg of beer over from the saloon. A cheer went up when he tapped it and sent a plume of foam into the air like a geyser.

"He's dead, and he took the hiding place with him," sobbed Belicia.

Slocum wasn't about to give up. He just didn't know what he was going to do to find the silver's hiding place.

19

"Now that's a strange request," the general store owner said, scratching his head. "Don't remember anyone asking that before."

"You do have maps of the area?" Slocum asked. He was growing impatient. He wanted out of Shakespeare as fast as possible. This wasn't his kind of town. The party went on out in the street and the gaiety mounted as the time for the stagecoach's arrival neared. There wasn't a one of the gathered citizens who didn't think it was a fine prank to play on the passengers.

Slocum wasn't sure what he'd think getting off a stagecoach after a long day's dusty ride and finding two men strung up inside the depot, but it wouldn't put him into a good mood.

"You have not heard of any such place?" Belicia pressed.

"I have a raft of maps, mostly left over from the days when there was something worth mining in the mountains," the shopkeeper said, "but there're a passel of places that start with the letters *s* and *k*."

Slocum leafed through the stack of maps, discarding most of them. He pushed three aside showing the twisting, turning canyons in the Peloncillo Mountains. Belicia ran her finger over the names printed in small letters.

"Here, John, here it is. Little Skull Canyon."

"Thought you said the name started with sk," the shopkeeper said. "That's most likely Skull Canyon. Or maybe it's Skeleton Canyon."

"There's a difference between Little Skull Canyon and Skull Canyon?" Slocum studied the maps, not finding either until the owner showed him.

"See here? This is Little Skull Canyon. Opened up a series of copper and silver mines there ten years back. Most petered out in a year or two, so the miners moved on."

"To Skull Canyon?"

"Can't rightly say that. Some might have, but Skull Canyon is way over here." He pointed to the far side of the map, representing a distance of more than twenty miles. "You only interested in those?"

"Why?" Slocum was growing more restive. He kept glancing at the door, sure the sheriff would show up with the shotgun and decided to hang a couple more for the town's amusement.

"Well, there's Ski Canyon. Gets real cold up in those mountains. And there's Skag Peak. Juts up like a knife."

"Any mining in those areas?" Belicia asked.

"There's mines everywhere. Not a one of them worth a plugged nickel," the shopkeeper said.

"We'll take these maps," Slocum said, forking over a few of the greenbacks he had stashed in his shirt pocket. The storekeeper scowled when he saw only paper money but said nothing, and offered no change for maps not worth fifty cents total.

"John, we—"

"Later, Belicia. We're getting out of Shakespeare right now." They went back into the street and dodged people dancing and singing. A second barrel of beer had been started and men were getting drunker by the minute. Presiding over it all like some medieval lord was the sheriff. He watched Slocum and Belicia as they returned to the jail and got their horses. Those cold eyes bothered Slocum, but what bothered him even more was the notion he'd never find the silver.

Jim Hughes had known these mountains well. All he needed was to find a petered out mine and dump the silver into it. Any shaft that had been worked longer than a month would be adequate to hide three tons of silver. Maybe a stick of dynamite to close it off, or maybe not even that. The Peloncillo Mountains were deserted now, all the metal ripped from its veins, the prospectors and miners gone.

"John, we can find it. We must. The statue—"

"Shut up and ride," he snapped. Slocum wasn't in a good mood. There were too many possibilities to explore, but the reward for success was great. Three tons of silver, and it'd all be his. Even sharing with Belicia, a ton of silver made him into a wealthy man.

They rode in silence for more than an hour, Slocum occasionally backtracking to be sure no one from Shakespeare trailed them. The sheriff and the townspeople were too busy with their grisly celebration. He and Belicia were free to look for the silver.

They stopped for a quick meal. Slocum spread the maps out on the ground and held the corners down with rocks to better study them. He scratched his head.

"Do you know where the silver is?" Belicia asked. "And the statue?"

"I heard Hughes mention Skeleton Canyon once. Can't remember exactly what he'd said about it. We're close by, and it's worth checking." He drew his finger along the winding canyon paths, trying to figure out where the Hughes Bunch might have traveled in the week between him going off with Belicia and the two of them reaching

Silver City. There were too many places within a fifty-mile area; the canyons twisted and turned and provided thousands of sites to hide the silver.

"You say he mentioned Skeleton Canyon? We are almost there! See! We are sure to find the silver and the statue."

Slocum wasn't so sure. He kept looking at the map, suspicion growing in him that Sandy King might have been choking out his last breath rather than trying to tell them the Hughes Bunch's hideout. He might have wanted King to tell him; he might have imagined the letters sk; he might have heard something else. The silver could be anywhere, and Slocum was sick with that realization.

Belicia sat and cooed to herself that the statue was nearby. Slocum tried to ignore her but couldn't. She was lovely but a touch of madness had entered her eyes. There was fire inside, but it was misdirected now and consuming her.

They finished their meal and rode to the mouth of Skeleton Canyon. Slocum stopped and looked at the pockmarked hills. Hundreds of spent mines lined the canyon walls, and the canyon snaked back into the mountains for miles.

"It's no good," Slocum said. "We'll never find it. The silver—and the statue—could be anywhere."

"But it is here. I feel it! It must be!" Belicia was flushed and shaking. "We cannot give up."

"The trail left by the burros is cold," Slocum said. "And they may have led the animals over into another canyon before releasing them, just to keep anyone tracking them from finding the hiding place. Even if they didn't, you could spend a lifetime searching just this canyon."

"The Virgin Mary is here!"

"Might be," Slocum allowed. "I might have heard wrong. King might have said something else, or it might have been nothing more than a death rattle." He sucked in a deep breath and released it slowly. New Mexico and Arizona were too hot for him right now. Going back into Mexico was out of the question with the *Federales* still searching for El Jéfe and the gringos who robbed the Monterrey mint.

If there was one chance in a million of finding the silver, Slocum would have looked. But there wasn't.

"I'm riding over into Texas," he said. "We'll never find the hiding place."

"I will never stop looking. She is here. She will guide me!" Slocum heard nothing but madness in her voice now. He wasn't going to spend his life hunting futilely for the silver.

Slocum rode for ten minutes, reached the canyon rim and looked back, hoping Belicia might have come to her senses and was riding to join him. He saw a small, dark figure near a mine shaft and knew how she'd spend her days.

He turned his mare's face and started east toward Texas. It'd be a week's ride, maybe more, before he got to El Paso. From there, he had no idea where he'd go.

Fury knew something was wrong long before he saw the wagon train spread out, unmoving, across the plains in front of him.

From miles away, he had noticed the cloud of dust kicked up by the hooves of the mules and oxen pulling the wagons. Then he had seen that tan-colored pall stop and gradually be blown away by the ceaseless prairie wind.

It was the middle of the afternoon, much too early for a wagon train to be stopping for the day. Now, as Fury topped a small, grass-covered ridge and saw the motionless wagons about half a mile away, he wondered just what kind of damn fool was in charge of the train.

Stopping out in the open without even forming into a circle was like issuing an invitation to the Sioux, the Cheyenne, or the Pawnee. War parties roamed these plains all the time just looking for a situation as tempting as this one.

Fury reined in, leaned forward in his saddle, and thought about it. Nothing said he had to go help those pilgrims. They might not even want his help. But from the looks of things, they needed his help, whether they wanted it or not.

He heeled the rangy lineback dun into a trot toward the wagons. As he approached, he saw figures scurrying back and forth around the canvas-topped vehicles. Looked sort of like an anthill after someone stomped it.

Fury pulled the dun to a stop about twenty feet from the lead wagon. Near it a man was stretched out on the ground with so many men and women gathered around him that Fury could only catch a glimpse of him through the crowd. When some of the men turned to look at him, Fury said, "Howdy. Thought it looked like you were having trouble."

"Damn right, mister," one of the pilgrims snapped. "And if you're of a mind to give us more, I'd advise against it."

Fury crossed his hands on the saddlehorn and shifted in the saddle, easing his tired muscles. "I'm not looking to cause trouble for anybody," he said mildly.

He supposed he might appear a little threatening to a bunch of immigrants who until now had never been any farther west than the Mississippi. Several days had passed since his face had known the touch of the razor, and his rough-hewn features could be a little intimidating even without the beard stubble. Besides that, he was well armed with a Colt's Third Model Dragoon pistol holstered on his right hip, a Bowie knife sheathed on his left, and a Sharps carbine in the saddleboot under his right thigh. And he had the look of a man who knew how to use all three weapons.

A husky, broad-shouldered six-footer, John Fury's height was apparent even on horseback. He wore a broad-brimmed, flat-crowned black hat, a blue work shirt, and fringed buckskin pants that were tucked into high-topped black boots. As he swung down from the saddle, a man's voice, husky with strain, called out, "Who's that? Who are you?"

The crowd parted, and Fury got a better look at the figure on the ground. It was obvious that he was the one who had spoken. There was blood on the man's face, and from the twisted look of him as he lay on the ground, he was busted up badly inside.

Fury let the dun's reins trail on the ground, confident that the horse wouldn't go anywhere. He walked over to the injured man and crouched beside him. "Name's John Fury," he said.

The man's breath hissed between his teeth, whether in pain or surprise Fury couldn't have said. "Fury? I heard of you."

Fury just nodded. Quite a few people reacted that way when they heard his name.

"I'm . . . Leander Crofton. Wagonmaster of . . . this here train." The man struggled to speak. He appeared to be in his fifties and had a short, grizzled beard and the leathery skin of a man who had spent nearly his whole life outdoors. His pale blue eyes were narrowed in a permanent squint.

"What happened to you?" Fury asked.

"It was a terrible accident— " began one of the men standing nearby, but he fell silent when Fury cast a hard glance at him. Fury had asked Crofton, and that was who he looked toward for the answer.

Crofton smiled a little, even though it cost him an effort. "Pulled a damn fool stunt," he said. "Horse nearly stepped on a rattler, and I let it rear up and get away from me. Never figured the critter'd spook so easy." The wagonmaster paused to draw a breath. The air rattled in his throat and chest. "Tossed me off and stomped all over me. Not the first time I been stepped on by a horse, but then a couple of the oxen pullin' the lead wagon got me, too, 'fore the driver could get 'em stopped."

"God forgive me, I . . . I am so sorry." The words came in a tortured voice from a small man with dark curly hair and a beard. He was looking down at Crofton with lines of misery etched onto his face.

"Wasn't your fault, Leo," Crofton said. "Just . . . bad luck."

Fury had seen men before who had been trampled by horses. Crofton was in a bad way, and Fury could tell by the look in the man's eyes that Crofton was well aware of it. The wagonmaster's chances were pretty slim.

"Mind if I look you over?" Fury asked. Maybe he could do something to make Crofton's passing a little easier, anyway.

One of the other men spoke before Crofton had a chance to answer. "Are you a doctor, sir?" he asked.

Fury glanced up at him, saw a slender, middle-aged man with iron-gray hair. "No, but I've patched up quite a few hurt men in my time."

"Well, I am a doctor," the gray-haired man said. "And I'd appreciate it if you wouldn't try to move or examine Mr. Crofton. I've already done that, and I've given him some laudanum to ease the pain."

Fury nodded. He had been about to suggest a shot of whiskey, but the laudanum would probably work better.

Crofton's voice was already slower and more drowsy from the drug as he said, "Fury . . ."

"Right here."

"I got to be sure about something . . . You said your name was . . . John Fury."

"That's right."

"The same John Fury who . . . rode with Fremont and Kit Carson?"

"I know them," Fury said simply.

"And had a run-in with Cougar Johnson in Santa Fe?"

"Yes."

"Traded slugs with Hemp Collier in San Antone last year?"

"He started the fight, didn't give me much choice but to finish it."

"Thought so." Crofton's hand lifted and clutched weakly at Fury's sleeve. "You got to . . . make me a promise."

Fury didn't like the sound of that. Promises made to dying men usually led to a hell of a lot of trouble.

Crofton went on, "You got to give me . . . your word . . . that you'll take these folks through . . . to where they're goin'."

"I'm no wagonmaster," Fury said.

"You know the frontier," Crofton insisted. Anger gave him strength, made him rally enough to lift his head from the ground and glare at Fury. "You can get 'em through. I know you can."

"Don't excite him," warned the gray-haired doctor.

"Why the hell not?" Fury snapped, glancing up at the physician. He noticed now that the man had his arm around the shoulders of a pretty red-headed girl in her teens, probably his daughter. He went on, "What harm's it going to do?"

The girl exclaimed, "Oh! How can you be so . . . so callous?"

Crofton said, "Fury's just bein' practical, Carrie. He knows we got to . . . got to hash this out now. Only chance we'll get." He looked at Fury again. "I can't make you promise, but it . . . it'd sure set my mind at ease while I'm passin' over if I knew you'd take care of these folks."

Fury sighed. It was rare for him to promise anything to anybody. Giving your word was a quick way of getting in over your head in somebody else's problems. But Crofton was dying, and even though they had never crossed paths before, Fury recognized in the old man a fellow Westerner.

"All right," he said.

A little shudder ran through Crofton's battered body, and he rested his head back against the grassy ground. "Thanks," he said, the word gusting out of him along with a ragged breath.

"Where are you headed?" Fury figured the immigrants could tell him, but he wanted to hear the destination from Crofton.

"Colorado Territory . . . Folks figure to start 'em a town . . . somewhere on the South Platte. Won't be hard for you to find . . . a good place."

No, it wouldn't, Fury thought. No wagon train journey could be called easy, but at least this one wouldn't have to deal with crossing mountains, just prairie. Prairie filled with savages and outlaws, that is.

A grim smile plucked at Fury's mouth as that thought crossed his mind. "Anything else you need to tell me?" he asked Crofton.

The wagonmaster shook his head and let his eyelids slide closed. "Nope. Figger I'll rest a spell now. We can talk again later."

"Sure," Fury said softly, knowing that in all likelihood, Leander Crofton would never wake up from this rest.

Less than a minute later, Crofton coughed suddenly, a wracking sound. His head twisted to the side, and blood welled for a few seconds from the corner of his mouth. Fury heard some of the women in the crowd cry out and turn away, and he suspected some of the men did, too.

"Well, that's all," he said, straightening easily from his kneeling position beside Crofton's body. He looked at the doctor. The red-headed teenager had her face pressed to the front of her father's shirt and her shoulders were shaking with sobs. She wasn't the only one crying, and even the ones who were dry-eyed still looked plenty grim.

"We'll have a funeral service as soon as a grave is dug," said the doctor. "Then I suppose we'll be moving on. You should know, Mr. . . . Fury, was it? You should know that none of us will hold you to that promise you made to Mr. Crofton."

Fury shrugged. "Didn't ask if you intended to or not. I'm the one who made the promise. Reckon I'll keep it."

He saw surprise on some of the faces watching him. All of these travelers had probably figured him for some sort of drifter. Well, that was fair enough. Drifting was what he did best.

But that didn't mean he was a man who ignored promises. He had given his word, and there was no way he could back out now.

He met the startled stare of the doctor and went on, "Who's the captain here? You?"

"No, I . . . You see, we hadn't gotten around to electing a captain yet. We only left Independence a couple of weeks ago, and we were all happy with the leadership of Mr. Crofton. We didn't see the need to select a captain."

Crofton should have insisted on it, Fury thought with a grimace. You never could tell when trouble would pop up. Crofton's body lying on the ground was grisly proof of that.

Fury looked around at the crowd. From the number of people standing there, he figured most of the wagons in the train were at least represented in this gathering. Lifting his voice, he said, "You all heard what Crofton asked me to do. I gave him my word I'd take over this wagon train and get it on through to Colorado Territory. Anybody got any objection to that?"

His gaze moved over the faces of the men and women who were standing and looking silently back at him. The silence was awkward and heavy. No one was objecting, but Fury could tell they weren't too happy with this unexpected turn of events.

Well, he thought, when he had rolled out of his soogans that morning, he hadn't expected to be in charge of a wagon train full of strangers before the day was over.

The gray-haired doctor was the first one to find his voice. "We can't speak for everyone on the train, Mr. Fury," he said. "But I don't know you, sir, and I have some reservations about turning over the welfare of my daughter and myself to a total stranger."

Several others in the crowd nodded in agreement with the sentiment expressed by the physician.

"Crofton knew me."

"He knew you to have a reputation as some sort of gunman!"

Fury took a deep breath and wished to hell he had come along after Crofton was already dead. Then he wouldn't be saddled with a pledge to take care of these people.

"I'm not wanted by the law," he said. "That's more than a lot of men out here on the frontier can say, especially those who have been here for as long as I have. Like I said, I'm not looking to cause trouble. I was riding along and minding my own business when I came across you people. There's too many of you for me to fight. You want to start out toward Colorado on your own, I can't stop you. But you're going to have to learn a hell of a lot in a hurry."

"What do you mean by that?"

Fury smiled grimly. "For one thing, if you stop spread out like this, you're making a target of yourselves for every Indian in these parts who wants a few fresh scalps for his lodge." He looked pointedly at the long red hair of the doctor's daughter. Carrie—that was what Crofton had called her, Fury remembered.

Her father paled a little, and another man said, "I didn't think there was any Indians this far east." Other murmurs of concern came from the crowd.

Fury knew he had gotten through to them. But before any of them had a chance to say that he should honor his promise to Crofton and take over, the sound of hoofbeats made him turn quickly.

A man was riding hard toward the wagon train from the west, leaning over the neck of his horse and urging it on to greater speed. The brim of his hat was blown back by the wind of his passage, and Fury saw anxious, dark brown features underneath it. The newcomer galloped up to the crowd gathered next to the lead wagon, hauled his lathered mount to a halt, and dropped lithely from the saddle. His eyes went wide with shock when he saw Crofton's body on the ground, and then his gaze flicked to Fury.

"You son of a bitch!" he howled.

And his hand darted toward the gun holstered on his hip.

If you enjoyed this book, subscribe now and get...

TWO FREE

A $7.00 VALUE–

If you would like to read more of the very best, most exciting, adventurous, action-packed Westerns being published today, you'll want to subscribe to True Value's Western Home Subscription Service.

Each month the editors of True Value will select the 6 very best Westerns from America's leading publishers for special readers like you. You'll be able to preview these new titles as soon as they are published, *FREE* for ten days with no obligation!

TWO FREE BOOKS

When you subscribe, we'll send you your first month's shipment of the newest and best 6 Westerns for you to preview. With your first shipment, two of these books will be yours as our introductory gift to you absolutely *FREE* (a $7.00 value), regardless of what you decide to do. If

you like them, as much as we think you will, keep all six books but pay for just 4 at the low subscriber rate of just $2.75 each. If you decide to return them, keep 2 of the titles as our gift. No obligation.

Special Subscriber Savings

When you become a True Value subscriber you'll save money several ways. First, all regular monthly selections will be billed at the low subscriber price of just $2.75 each. That's at least a savings of $4.50 each month below the publishers price. Second, there is never any shipping, handling or other hidden charges—*Free home delivery*. What's more there is no minimum number of books you must buy, you may return any selection for full credit and you can cancel your subscription at any time. A TRUE VALUE!